The Lost Protector

Book Three of The Unity Chronicles

GRAHAM MANN

The Lost Protector

Book Three of The Unity Chronicles

Prologue

A dart-like vessel pierced the light grey sky and made a swift descent to the surface of the ice planet. The sleek vessel was clearly of Raktarian design, finished in highly reflective chrome and translucent red. The immaculately polished surface reflected the planet's glacial terrain in spectacular detail. From above, this unwelcoming world appeared to be completely uninhabitable. However, a vast underground system of dwellings and research laboratories sprawled beneath the planet's desolate snow-covered landscape. The lack of hospitable outdoor areas is what led to the introverted, studious evolution of the Raktarian race. The people of Raktar hadn't engaged with The Unity since before the activation of the Unity Spire. No one knew if it was through shame at the weapons that they had created, a lack of interest, or for other unknown reasons...

A sharp hiss sounded, and the seamlessly concealed door of the craft opened. It twisted and lowered to become a boarding ramp. A tall figure stepped out from the doorway and pulled up the faux fur hood of his bulky-padded jacket, in order to protect his head and face from the wind and cold. His heavy boots made a metallic clang with every footfall. He walked the length of the ramp to reach terra-firma.

The crunch and squeak of the thick snow underfoot was a brand-new experience, as were the delicate flurries of flakes that whipped around him.

Five frustrating years had passed, and Taire was no closer to finding the sixth child of The Unity. Once the dust had settled on the battle of Mora, Tecta had exiled himself. He had given the command - which in turn had led to the obliteration of Feer'aal. He did it to bolster The Unity's chances of beating Injis. But, ever since that day, he had felt like more of a risk than a benefit to the fledgling Unity. He had never thought of himself as being capable of such extremes. Tecta had broken his own rules and believed that he had condemned his cybernetic soul to damnation. He had even compared himself to Injis and Rarvin. He alone was of this opinion; the rest of the new Unity knew that he had done what was necessary to protect them, and if he hadn't of taken those actions, it was highly doubtful that any of them would still be alive today.

The sudden disappearance of his mechanized father figure had affected Taire deeply, right down to his core, even more so than it had his siblings. Taire still had the Sixth to find, and Tecta had always been there to be his friend, mentor and confidant. Now Lu and Gliis had additional companions in Tam and Kee'Pah respectively, he felt more alone than ever before. He needed Tecta's guidance desperately, but Tecta wasn't here. He was out there alone, unreachable, enduring his self-imposed exile in the vast expanse of space. Taire followed Etala's advice. He had taken it upon himself to search for the answers, but he had repeatedly drawn a complete blank. In the years since the activation of the Unity Spire, Taire had avoided coming to Raktar. Although it was his native planet, he'd never felt the urge, or the calling, to come here before. He had exhausted all other avenues. In a fit of hope and desperation, he had concluded that in order to find the answer within himself, he needed to know more about his identity, his people and his heritage. He needed to find out who Taire truly was. An electronic trilling sounded to his right-hand side. It was the now familiar complaining of Clint, his homemade companion. The name Clint was an abbreviation of the tech he had been built around. *Conscious LearnINg Technology*. Clint had strayed out of his depth in the thick snow. His boosters roared like miniature blow torches. They melted the surrounding snow and lifted him above the drift, and onto the comparative safety of the boarding ramp. He landed with a gentle clank and trilled some more.

"Yes Clint, I know it's cold, stop complaining. I programmed you to be my companion and sounding board, not a nagging stand-in for a life partner." Clint gave a negative bleep.

"Fine, you just sulk. I didn't have to bring you along. You insisted, remember?" Clint gave a blunt *nurng* sound, hovered up to Taire's kit bag, and nestled himself inside.

"*Sorry?* So, you should be." Taire couldn't quite believe that it had come to this. He had receded so far into himself that he had resorted to building a companion, rather than being around actual people. He knew Lu, Gliis, Tam and Kee'Pah hadn't meant to exclude him, and a large part of the problem was that he had distanced himself from them. He had gotten lost in his introverted search for the Sixth. Even Treelo had left on some mission to the darker parts of the galaxy. He was now a self-appointed ambassador for the New Unity. With a limitless supply of credits for his trouble, he fanatically spread the word of "peace" wherever he went.

In any case, Taire had grown very fond of Clint, and although at times he was infuriated by him, he did provide companionship and a welcome distraction. As Taire regarded his surroundings, he rubbed his hands together to create some warming friction. He had purposefully chosen this spot to land his ship. He had it on good authority that this was the most accessible landing platform on Raktar; although his current semi-frozen state had caused him to question the reliability of his sources. It was clear to see - there was nothing here. No dwellings or research sites, no people, just the crunch of the snow, and the howl and whistle of the wind that hurried the gentle flakes of snow about the icy outcrops.

Taire was startled by a sudden jolt underfoot, it was accompanied by a new sound. The sound was mechanical - it resembled the grinding of heavy gear plates. Taire became aware of the sensation of motion. He, Clint and his ship were being slowly rotated and lowered into the planet's surface. Clint gave a panicked trill.

    "Don't worry little friend, these are my people."

Chapter One

Antipathy

"Well, where is this magnificent Mech-Warrior?" the withered serpentine tones of God's voice slithered through the air. She regarded the holographic footage before her with a greedy intrigue.

"We have gathered much information and traced its origins to the Second System, exalted one," Shaar responded.

"Hsssss, the Second System? If that is so, how was this recording found this far out?"

"We are yet to ascertain this; it could be leaked black-market footage, or fate perhaps?" Shaar's tone lay somewhere between desperate and hopeful.

"You are well aware of my lack of patience when I see something that I wish to possess, are you not Shaar?" God spoke in hissed whispers.

"Oh, gracious one, I pledge to you on my honour, I will find the Mech and deliver it to you," Shaar answered. The anxiety in his voice grew audibly.

"Why would you dare to tease such savage delights, when you have no means to deliver them to me?" Throughout the duration of the exchange, God's tone had shifted from intrigue to delight, then completely bypassed annoyance, to skip to complete rage.

"Daa'Shond!" she roared with deafening ferocity.

"Yes, my glorious God?" grovelled Daa'Shond.

"Cast this disappointment into the arena... The stench of his fear is nauseating, his mere presence offends my senses."

"No! have mercy, I beg you. I will find it. I swear to you." Shaar pleaded, but it was to no avail.

"Against whom shall he do battle with my lady?" asked Daa'Shond. A vicious grin dominated his face - he was enjoying this a little too much.

"Kaa'lash the Abominator feels like the correct opponent. I'm in the mood for some limb separation."

"Excellent choice," said Daa'Shond, who rubbed his palms together in anticipation.

"No! please…" cried Shaar.

"Pitiful - if you are that desperate to live, you simply need to win the fight." Daa'Shond gave a mockingly pinched laugh. He knew that Shaar was no warrior; he was and always had been no more than a seeker. Shaar kicked and screamed in panic as he was dragged out to the arena below them by one of God's many servile hybrid sectoid units.

* * * * * * * * *

"Huh Hum" Daa'Shond cleared his throat. He plucked the announcing mic from its cradle, with his pincer-like fingers and thumb.

"Fellow patrons of the battle rock Antipathy, may I have your attention." His voice thin and distorted, it echoed through the honeycomb of tunnels and cells, to the farthest reaches of the battle rock.

"Thanks to our gracious God. We have an unscheduled treat for your blood-thirsty viewing pleasure. Our very own groveling little snot Shaar, has whetted our saviour's appetite, with images of a most savage mech-warrior. Alas, Shaar has failed dismally to deliver this warrior to our lady God. Such a bitter disappointment." He tutted and shook his head. "In order to put the scowl back on our glorious God's face, Shaar will be doing battle with none other than the reigning champion, Kaa'Lash the Abominator. The booths are open, place your bets now."

Roars and cries of approval penetrated the thick walls and swelled in the vast corridors of Antipathy. No matter what they were doing, the many varied beings that inhabited the colony, immediately dropped everything to head to the arena. It was an insane race to place their wagers and get to the best vantage points of the arena. Predictably, fights broke out in the crush of bodies. These fights became casual betting opportunities. Anyone that was pushed free of the tidal surge and press of beings, would brandish their credits to get a piece of this lower key action. The place was like Wonk'aat station on acid.

The dimly-lit betting booths lined the outer walls of the arena. They were alive with the throng of beings of all shapes and sizes, jostling to reach the front of their respective lines... desperate to place their wagers. Bong!! The ancient gong sounded - you could almost hear the dust that flew from it as its deep tone penetrated the arena, bringing with it a unified hush. The betting booth shutters slammed down violently.

"Betting is closed, take your seats for the main event in five...four..three..two..one! Please welcome to the arena our once beloved friend and allies, who has become nought but a saddening disappointment, Shaar!!" Shaar was thrust out from an opening in the wall of the arena. His boney head hung low; he was the image of a defeated being. A gangly broken thing. He didn't even bother to plead any further for God's forgiveness. The crowd booed and jeered, while God herself watched on from up high. The arena had been built around her nest within the rock's core - she was an impressively massive Sectoid. Over the many years that she had existed here, (too many for her to even recall), her physical being had melded with the rock itself, rendering her a part of the structure. Her features were obscured in shadow, except for her bright yellow eyes, which cut through the gloom of the upper portion of the arena. Those eyes glared, unblinking, down on to the battleground in anticipation.

"Shaar! Choose your weapons," commanded Daa'Shond, through the static of the tannoy. Shaar's rage at Daa'Shond's voice had spurred him on to at least try to fight, he knew he had zero chance of a reprieve from God. He needed to save his energy and use his cunning to give himself the best chance he could. With this in mind, he selected distance weapons, blasters, grenades and a jetpack. If Kaa'Lash couldn't catch him, he couldn't tear his limbs off. He glared up at the announcer's box as he primed the blasters.
"Damn you Daa'Shond, someday you'll fall out of favour and it'll be you down here,"

Shaar shouted, his words laced with venom.

"Mwah!! How charming," laughed Daa'Shond. "Shall we welcome the reigning champion?"

"YES! YES! YES!" came the collective cries of the crowd. "Kaa'Lash, Kaa'Lash, Kaa'Lash!" The chants grew in volume, accompanied by rhythmic feet, stomping and hand clapping. The noise swelled to become a primal chant.

"Friends...and you Shaar, please welcome the undisputed champion of Antipathy. The one, the only... KAA'LASH THE ABOMINATOR!!" Frenzied screams and whooping sounds filled the arena as Kaa'Lash made his entrance.

The gargantuan Sectacoil rolled intimidatingly slowly onto the arena. The dusty-gritty ground crunched and creaked under the enormous weight of its armoured shell. Shaar had backed as far away from the approaching sphere of horror as possible. He had seen Kaa'Lash fight on a number of occasions and the memory of each didn't do much to bolster his already shaky confidence. He knew he had to time this to perfection. He fitted the jet pack and charged his blasters. The slowly rolling boulder of shell grew ever closer to Shaar. If he could force Kaa'Lash to open its shell before it was ready, he might have a slither of an opportunity to attack. The menacing sphere of terror stopped and Shaar took two purposeful steps forward. Then it happened... the piercing scream of Kaa'Lash's shell vents. Shaar hurled grenades at him, they stuck fast to the mammoth shell and detonated instantly. Kaa'Lash's shell was forced prematurely open by the blast; its muscular, wiry limbs unfurled. They were at least fifteen feet long, built of solid muscle and sinew. Shaar opened fire. He knew he couldn't pierce

the shell, and attacking Kaa'Lash's opened
form was his best and only shot. He engaged
the jet pack - it propelled him backwards,
diagonally and upward. He unleashed bolt after
bolt of blaster fire, interspersed with yet
more grenades. There was so much smoke, dust
and debris that he couldn't see if his assault
had made any impact. He found out soon enough,
a thrashing limb burst out from the smoke,
followed by another and yet another. Shaar
managed to evade the first wave of attacks, by
the slimmest of margins, skillfully thrusting
and cutting his jets in extreme manoeuvres.
His head swam from the motion, but he couldn't
lose concentration. He resumed firing his
blasters, and reached for another grenade, but
he was completely out.

The full horror of Kaa'Lash's form came into
view as the dust and smoke thinned. This
wasn't a fair match up. It was like pitting a
wasp against a Kraken. Shaar felt like he was
hovering over a chaotic, swirling hellstorm
and Kaa'Lash's giant eye was its centre, a
pure black abyss... devoid of emotion,
surrounded by those deadly flailing limbs.
Shaar concentrated all of his firepower on the
eye. It was like a highly polished boulder of
blackest granite. The shots were futile, every
bolt ricocheted then fizzled out. Shaar's
blasters were out of charge, he knew he had no
chance now. His ears grew deaf to the cries of
the crowd, they became muffled and faded. The
only sound that remained were his shallow
breaths and the rapid pounding of his own
heart sending his blood racing through his
veins. Shaar let out a defiant scream and
powered towards Kaa'Lash... *If I can't defeat
it I will at least deny it the pleasure of*

tearing me limb from limb. Shaar's rocket-fuelled descent was fast, but Kaa'Lash's reflexes were like lightning. Shaar was trapped staring down at his doomed reflection in that deep mirror-like black eye, the image confirmed the grim truth that he was already crushingly aware of: he had totally and utterly failed and was about to pay the ultimate price. His wrists, ankles and neck were all in the grasp of Kaa'Lash's powerful limbs. They held him outstretched and taught until the last of the jet fuel burned away. The crowd grew silent and waited for the grand finale. The deafening silence was broken by the sickening crack and squelch of Shaar's body being savagely dismembered. The short-sharp sound of his demise echoed around the arena. In a ferocious spin, Shaar's severed limbs were flung to the corners of the arena, and his torso fell to the dusty ground with a thud. Kaa'Lash swiped a solid limb at Shaar's severed head, which launched it high into the air. One of God's many serrated pincers darted out from the gloom and skewered the head from back to front, the tip of her pincer burst through Shaar's forehead. She admired the precision of her aim for a second, then gave a satisfied hiss. She tossed the head into the frenzied mess of the crowd. The heads of the fallen were valuable trophies; Shaar's head would be ferociously fought over, before finding its proud new owner.

"Show your appreciation for the most vicious of our champions, KAA'LASH THE ABOMINATOR!!" The crowd shrieked and cheered; their chants rose once more as Kaa'Lash performed its trademark dizzying victory spin.
"Hold fast friends, all must hear what I

have to say. Our gracious lady God has
instructed me to issue a potentially lucrative
challenge to all. Watch what I am about to
show you, very closely."

A holographic projection of a Warrior-Mech
illuminated the centre of the arena. The
gathered watched in silent awe as they
witnessed images of a Mech totally decimating
four, viciously well-trained, assassins. It
was a fiercely contested battle of strategy,
fire power and hand-to-hand combat. The Mech
was the epitome of what a warrior should be.
Merciless, fearless and resilient - it adapted
to overcome every eventuality to emerge the
worthy victor.
    "The Mech in this footage is the object of
our God's desire. She wishes to possess him,
and to put him into battle in the arena." At
this point, Kaa'Lash, who was unimpressed by
what it saw as an inferior tin man in the
hologram, retreated into its shell and
casually rolled off the arena.
    "The only information we have on this Mech
is that he originates from the Second System,
and that he is known by the name Tecta. Such
is our lady God's desire to own this warrior,
whomever delivers him to her, will never want
for anything ever again. The betting booths
are open once more. If you do not wish to
actively seek the Mech, you can always place a
bet on who his captors will be. Keep your eyes
trained on the booths for the latest odds and
retain the bragging rights that come with
being part of the most infamous warrior hunt
in recorded... no, *all* of history. Friends,
sign up now to join the hunt for this
formidable adversary, or...if you don't have
the stones... stay home, place your bets, and

watch it all unfold. Mwah!"

Chapter Two

Tecta's Ascent

Planet Unity five years earlier:

The familiar trek seemed to take so much longer than it ever had before, it was akin to wading through syrupy Granyox drool, each step seemingly taking a herculean effort. Tecta had felt this heavy mess of emotions before, back on Veela VI, when he knew he had to send the siblings away. He had hoped he would never have to experience these feelings again, but it was unavoidable, he had to leave.

He thought of the siblings now, on what could be his last ever walk on his beloved planet Unity. His thoughts of the three children he had raised filled him with pride. He was confident that they would be okay, and he had no doubt that ultimately, they would succeed in their mission. On the eve of the battle of Mora, Nataalu had told him that they would need his help and guidance to forge a path to the future, not least to help them make sense of the cryptic clues that had been presented to them. Firstly, by the Eye of Veela, and then there were the mysteries hidden within the words Etala Maas had spoken to them at the Unity Spire. With the addition of Tam and

Kee'Pah, the Children of The Unity were now five in number. They were strong and wise beyond their collective years. He would not jeopardise their futures with any more of his misguided interference. Etala had tasked Taire with finding the sixth child of The Unity. Taire was bright, probably the brightest of them all, and Tecta was confident that he would fulfil his task. It was just a matter of time and patience.

Tecta's thoughts grew dark once more. He could add coward to the list of self-deprecating things he now believed himself to be. He couldn't even summon the courage to say goodbye to his beloved children. The mere thought of it, bidding farewell to the three reasons his life had meaning, the ones he had raised from infancy, was too much for him to bear. He hoped that one day they would understand why he had no choice but to leave. He had ordered the attack on the Feruccian home world to aid The Unity in their conflict with Injis; ultimately that order had led to the destruction of the planet's entire population. When Tecta had given the command, a darkness had infiltrated him, and he couldn't run the risk of that darkness infecting the New Unity. Tecta longed for those early years on Veela VI with the young siblings. It was no wonder he had been so reluctant to let them leave. Almost everything before and after those few precious years had been war and chaos.

He had finally reached the summit. The newly restored Unity Spire stood boldly at the crest of the mountain. This journey was at an end. He took a long last look at his surroundings,

the majestic mountains, with their subtle
tones of red and slate grey. They took on a
purple hue in the evening shadows cast by the
setting sun, as it made its descent to the
horizon. He bid farewell to the purple and
pink haze that reflected from the underside of
the light wisps of cloud, and beyond those,
the majesty of the Broken Crown, as it took
its place in the magnificent evening sky.
Tecta placed his arms by his sides and
triggered his internal countdown. He became
the inanimate metal sarcophagus that all
Protectors transformed into when engaging
hibernation protocols. All power diverted to
his boosters and he was transformed into a
space bound projectile. With a mighty blast,
he headed up through the scant cloud cover,
and became a tiny speck in the vast Unitian
sky. The last rays of the sun glinted from his
reflective casing. A sonic boom sounded in his
wake, and he disappeared into the darkness
beyond the planet's atmosphere.

Chapter Three

The Hunt

Seven Hundred and Seventy lunar passes ago till now

The race to find Tecta was on. God had deployed her own seeker teams to inject a little urgency into proceedings. The rabble of miscreants that had poured out of Antipathy to search for her prize, were mostly less than dynamic. For centuries, God's Seeker Drones had scoured the furthest reaches of space, to find fighters worthy of the honour that was doing battle on Antipathy. Tecta was their latest, and possibly greatest, prey.

The Seeker Drones were relentless and unscrupulous in their pursuit, and Daa'Shond was only too aware of this. He would use them to his advantage. For weeks he had tracked them from a comfortable distance, listening in on their progress, whilst they had tracked subspace transmissions, news networks; even listening in on their casual conversations and researched rumours and urban myths. All in their pursuit of the formidable Warrior Droid. Midway through the fifth week, at the point Daa'Shond thought he may be losing the will to live, Seeker team Centauri made the big breakthrough. They extrapolated the relevant information and mapped out a search quadrant. The location they pinpointed was perilous. Tecta was in the midst of the intersection between Liquid Space and Dead Space, on the cusp of a Z-class black hole. The black hole was in its infancy, but still powerful enough to drag the two incompatible forms of space together and in towards itself. This effect caused the formation of a deceptively beautiful, tentacle-like tendril. The unmixable space matter swirled and bubbled as it struggled to break free from one another. It was stunning to behold. If Tecta was conscious, he would've marvelled at such a sight: but as it stood, he was oblivious, entombed in the metal sarcophagus of his own hibernated body. Daa'Shond's sneaky monitoring of the subspace exchanges between God and the drones had paid off. Once he had learned Tecta's whereabouts, he disrupted the Seeker Drone's transmission feeds, and wasted no time in launching a stealth attack on the unwitting drones. Daa'Shond obliterated them with consummate ease. Of course, it helped that he knew the Seeker's shield modulation frequencies and their weak spots. He pinpointed these exact areas; the impact of his attacks caused instantaneous, critical damage. He showed no remorse for his contemptible actions. He simply mag-locked onto the oblivious Tecta's casing and headed for Antipathy. Daa'Shond had done it - he had sneakily snatched ultimate glory from the drones and had ensured he would be enshrined in legend. It would be him that collected the prize for capturing the mighty Tecta. With all the ambient interference that was being

generated by the black hole, no one would ever
find out what really happened here.

* * * * * * * * * *

Tecta was groggy and aware that he was being
forcefully awoken.
*'Can I not get some peace?! Even as I drift
untethered in the vast expanse of space,
somehow, someone, has managed to seek me out'.*
He became acutely aware that he was being
watched, and he was definitely no longer in
space.

"Ahh! Splendid! You're awake," a pinched
voice spoke. Tecta opened his eyes. He
regarded the creature that sat opposite him
with an uncharacteristic disdain. The laser
bars of his cell crackled and glowed, creating
a lethal barrier between the two of them.

"Allow me to introduce myself. I am
Daa'Shond." The creature was an annoyingly
well-spoken being, not to mention smug-
sounding. His voice was so piercingly high-
pitched and nasal, that Tecta momentarily
debated shutting off his aural processors. He
would've done it in a milli-second, if he
wasn't so disorientated. He was at a distinct
disadvantage and needed answers.

"Where am I?" he asked.

"You are on the battle rock of Antipathy,
in the Korrix system," Daa'Shond responded.

"Never heard of it. How did I come to be
here?"

"I salvaged you - now you are my property.
Though not for long, as you are to be my gift
to God. She does love an extravagant present."

"I am no one's property, and I will not be
anyone's gift!" Tecta replied angrily.

"Any object, appliance or craft which does

not possess the power or will to self-propel and/or is found to be adrift, abandoned, discarded or otherwise stranded - shall be deemed the property of the finder." Daa'Shond recited the passage from the universal Salvage Law.

"You friend, at the time of my discovery, fell into these categories. Besides, you should be thanking me. You were drifting perilously close to a black hole when I found you."

"You should have left me there."

"Oh my, a suicidal droid. How...quirky!" Tecta refused to respond, instead he asked another question.

"So, do you mean to kill me, or dissect me? What are your intentions?"

"We are not savages here, and we have big plans for you. You see, we simply enjoy the thrill of extremes, and you my friend are about to partake in the most extreme of all sports. It is a popular notion that you are going to be the perfect participant."

"Is that so?" scoffed Tecta.

"Yes, I am very confident that is so. You *will* be taking part. You see, the stakes are set oh so very high to further enhance the experience. Some of the best fighting species are quite the dullard type, so we've kept the rules very simple. In the arena, you will kill or be killed. However, your suicidal mind-set tells me that you wouldn't put up much of a fight. You'd embrace being killed, and where's the entertainment value in that? So, if you won't fight for your life, maybe you'll fight to save your precious Unity." Mocked Daa'Shond with his irritatingly pinched laugh.

"Mmwah." The sound resembled the pretentious false kisses that theatrical types greet each other with. They usually pre-empt these air kisses with an overly drawn out version of the word darling. The sound filled Tecta with the urge to smash Daa'Shond's smug, pointy face in.

"You do not possess that kind of power!" He spat.

"Indeed, I don't, but God does." He paused and gave Tecta a psychotic grin.

"Oh yes, speaking of God. She wants to know why you don't look our image of you in the battle archives. Actually, we would all like to know." Daa'Shond glared with such intensity, it appeared that he was trying to pierce Tecta's mind, in an attempt to read his thoughts. His devious shark-like eyes were black and emotionless as he casually sat and filed his razor-sharp teeth, waiting for Tecta's response. For a being of such illustrious airs and graces, this type of public grooming seemed wholly inappropriate.

"It's a long story" said Tecta, after an uncomfortably long pause.

"Who, may I ask, is God?" His tone carried his disdain openly.

"Such a profound question from a Mech, Mwah!!" He did his pinched laugh again.

"God is the chosen name of the glorious being that presides over Antipathy. God has always lived here, Queen of the original hive. Now she provides for us, so that we may in return deliver to her the gift of entertainment. Entertainment of which you are now a part. Welcome to the circus, Tecta."

"If I am to be kept here as a prisoner, I ask you to call me by my formal denomination, RPU Fourteen."

"That's a bit clinical... don't you think

dear boy? Not very, well, showbiz. How about we call you The Iron Bear. In battle, your brutality is savage as a wild animal, and you *are* constructed of metallic compounds. The masses will adore such a name, and in this place, if you do not have the crowds on side, you have nothing my friend."

"Call me what you will, with the exclusion of my actual name, and let me be clear... we are not friends!"

"Oh, *excuse me*, but we'll see about that. You will need a friend here soon enough. Mwah!"

"I doubt that, and I would like to add that I am not comprised of anything as low grade as iron," snapped Tecta.

"Such self-assured, misplaced arrogance. Let me be crystal clear, If you refuse to fight, The Unity dies. If you try to escape, The Unity dies. If you don't do exactly as you are told…"

"Let me guess, The Unity dies?" Tecta's voice was laced with frustration and an aggressive sarcasm.

"Good good, you are a fast learner. Your first fight takes place in the morning. So prepare yourself in any way that you choose, just be ready, Mwah! I'm afraid for the moment you will have to excuse me, I have a prior dinner engagement. Two live Granyox await my freshly-filed teeth. I will leave you to ponder that which we have discussed."

"Please, take your time," Tecta sneered. As Daa'Shond walked away, he paused and glanced back at his captive.

"One more thing. If you adore your beloved Unity so much, then why did you leave?"

"A creature such as you would never understand."

"That may be so, but I do understand exactly who and what I am. Can you, in all honesty, say the same?" With a cocked eyebrow, and a flash of his razor-sharp grin, Daa'Shond resumed his exit; leaving Tecta, head hung low, to contemplate his question.

Chapter Four

Son of Raktar I

The rotating platform eased to a halt. Taire and Clint found themselves in a subterranean hangar. Their surroundings were lit in a soft-white glow which radiated from the creases where the walls met the ceiling. A Raktarian male approached - Taire thought him to be a little older than himself. The man wore a humourless expression and a stiff smile.

"Greetings Taire, I am Reynar. We have been waiting for you to come home."

"*Really?!!*" Taire replied, finding it hard to mask his surprise. "The new Unity have heard nothing from Raktar. We thought you wished to have no part in what we are building." Taire's words appeared to wound Reynar.

"No...nothing could be further from the truth. You needed to come here of your own volition, when you were ready. We are not worthy to intervene or coerce you in any way." Reynar gave his stiff smile again.

"Where are my manners? You must be hungry and thirsty. Everyone here is very eager to meet you. Please come." Reynar gestured for them to follow.

He led them through a series of claustrophobic corridors, then into a mess-hall-of-sorts.

There were twenty or so people of varying ages gathered inside, eyes wide in wonder at their first glimpse of the famous Taire, Raktarian child of The Unity. The anticipation was palpable. A humble spread had been prepared for them; it was very functional - protein pods, synthetic meats and vitamin-enriched drinks. It was far from adventurous, but in all honesty, he hadn't expected anything at all. Taire had been greeted by his people with open arms. They were friendly and very accomodating; not one person had asked why he had never visited his home world before, although many had said they had always hoped that one day he would honour them with his presence. The Raktarians wanted to hear the stories of his adventures, the battles, the Unity Spire: anything and everything about him. A Raktarian child, about ten years of age, approached Taire and tugged at his tunic.

"Please Pure One, can you show me how to be like you when I am grown?" said the child. Taire knelt so that he was eye-to-eye with the child.

"What is your name?" Taire asked.

"Rylar," the child replied.

"Well Rylar, we all have our own path, and we must all find our own way. I'm certain that yours will be one that's bold and adventurous. You have a very curious nature." The child smiled, before being aggressively snatched away by an Elder.

"Apologies, Pure One," said the Elder.

"There's no need to apologise, he is just being a curious child." Taire replied.

"He asks too many questions."

"Isn't that how we all learn? I have many questions myself. That is one of the reasons that I am here."

"Of course, and we are all very happy to assist you in anyway that we can. We have nothing to hide here," the Elder smiled uncomfortably, and hurried the child Rylar away...
Something about the whole place felt amiss, false and sterile. Taire was sensing an uncomfortable, underlying air of secrecy.

"Come friends, we must let our homecoming son rest and unwind. There will be time for stories later."

"Reynar, I don't wish to seem rude or forward, but I have heard that the archives that you have, housed here on Raktar, date back to our earliest origins. I am keen to know more of our world and my own lineage. Would it be possible for me to access them?"

"Of course, Taire, but do you not wish to rest? The archives will still be here in the morning," Reynar replied.

"To be honest, I'm not much of a sleeper, and after the excitement of your warm welcome, my mind is abuzz with questions."

"Of course," said Reynar, and sharply clapped his hands twice. The gathered Raktarians jumped to attention and hurriedly began to tidy the refreshments away. Taire didn't have the chance to thank them, he was ushered away so swiftly by Reynar.

"The archives are this way, you are free to access all of our files. We have nothing to hide here." Reynar's words were measured and his tone level. Taire was suspicious about the number of times he'd heard the words 'We have nothing to hide here' since his arrival. Several of the people present at the welcoming party had also said the exact same sentence. Not least of all young Rylar's chaperone. This

only added to the nagging misgivings that
nibbled at his subconscious mind.

Reynar gestured towards a short, starkly-lit
hallway and led Taire into a small room. It
was clinical, lined in polished metal. He
really had expected more, something ancient
and mystical maybe, but this was compact and
of course highly efficient. A single reading
station stood in the centre of the sterile
room.
    "From this station you can view our
history in its entirety. Well, from the time
records began. Our complete archives are
stored within these four walls."
    "Very...economical," smiled Taire.
    "I will leave you to your research. If you
need anything, please just ask."
    "Thank you for your hospitality Reynar."
    "You are most welcome, my brother. You
are, after all, a fellow son of Raktar, and
unquestionably the most famous of us all."
Reynar left the room and sealed the door
behind him.
    "See, I told you Clint, these are my
people". Taire's tone was that of a man trying
to convince himself that his own words were
true. But Clint wasn't buying it. He gave a
wary groan in reply - he didn't like Reynar,
or anything else about this place.

Taire activated the station and began to feel
his way around the archives. The interface was
extremely advanced; it utilised the thoughts
and impulses of the user, in order to guide
them to the sections of the files that they
most desired to explore. It wasn't long before
Clint set his system to sleep/surveillance
mode. He had grown bored of watching Taire sit

in silence with that blank expression on his face. A function of the interface, unbeknown to Taire, was to raise susceptibility. His mind had been opened to suggestion and was being flooded with more than just the archives. A voice entered his mind, at first it was a faint whisper, an unintelligible background chatter, then it grew and swelled to a deep commanding tone. His subconscious rationalised it, he must be dreaming, dreams triggered by what he was seeing in the archives.

"Child of Raktar, you must fulfil your birthright. You must find and wake me, your one true god." It was an order... not a request. The voice filled his mind, it was a cruel, chilling voice that bought with it a feeling of overwhelming fear and malevolence.

"You will serve only me," the voice continued.

"Wake, Pure One." A new gentle voice entered Taire's mind, cutting through the thick dark fog that had invaded his thoughts. Clint sensed something was wrong, as Taire's stress levels and stats were rising rapidly. His eyelids twitched and flickered unnaturally. Clint shrieked and nudged him, bleeping wildly. Taire wouldn't stir. In a state of desperation, Clint zapped Taire with a static charge. He sat bolt upright, his face coated in beads of cold sweat and his eyes wide with panic. The new voice from Taire's dream-like state was still speaking. It was here in the physical realm, and it was coming from beyond the sealed door.

"Reject them Pure One, and their false Goddess. She means to use you for your power." Taire pushed the door. They were locked in.

"Summon your gifts and find me. I can give

you the truths that you seek."

Taire felt a raw power penetrating his body, he instinctively knew it was the essence of the planet surging within him. It rose through the ground and pulsed through every fibre of his being. He focused on the door and held his hands out in front of him, exactly as he had done with his siblings at the Unity Spire. The energy rushed within him, like a fire in his blood. Taire drew his hands back to his chest, then thrust them forward, unleashing a powerful blast of energy. The sealed door squealed, creaked and burst open. A mess of burred molten metal was all that remained.

　　"Come on Clint, we need to leave." Clint squealed impatiently.
"No, I don't know what's happening or where we're going, we just need to get away from here, now!"

Chapter Five

Fight One

Tecta was led through a series of corridors by a bizarre looking pair of hybrid Sectoids. They weren't much for conversation, but Tecta didn't mind that. He was feeling far from chatty. As they approached the gateway to the arena, he could see Daa'Shond waiting for them.

"Good morning Bear," Daa'Shond addressed Tecta.

"Is it?" came the less than enthusiastic response.

"So glad to see you didn't try some ill-conceived escape."

"You make it sound like I have a choice," sneered Tecta.

"Oh my dear boy, there is always a choice, Mwah!" Daa'Shond gave an ugly smirk, "I just wanted to wish you luck. I expect a good show. I'll be up in the gods, in the luxury seats. Do give me a wave." Tecta didn't dignify Daa'Shond's comments with a reply, but there was no escaping his smug voice.

"Beloved allies, fiends and deviants." Daa'Shond's irritating tone filled the air, it ground on Tecta like grains of sand between his teeth. "Our first contestant, you all love to loathe him! Welcome Meld!!" Boos echoed throughout the crowd. Meld was an unpopular

fighter. He had beaten every opponent he'd
ever faced, inside of a minute. Not good value
for money and the odds were useless.
Daa'Shond's plan was to make Tecta an instant
favourite, to prove to God that he had
provided her with the ultimate fighter. "And
now, all the way from the Second System, the
master of metallic mayhem, I give you the
Indestructible Iron Bear."

Tecta stomped heavily into the arena. The air
was thick with second-hand reed smoke and the
ground was warm and wet underfoot. He looked
about the barren space. *Where is he?* Meld had
been announced first, so he should have
already been in the arena. Tecta took two more
steps... his aural processors detected a faint
groaning. He stomped down hard with his right
foot and a sound, akin to a sharp exhalation,
came from nearby. The crowd began to laugh as
water began to rise from the dank ground, it
clung to Tecta's ankles and began to creep
eerily up his legs. Tecta activated his flame-
throwers and directed the blasts of fire
towards his lower half. Plumes of steam hissed
and rose into the air. The remaining water ran
from his legs and pooled a few metres away. A
column of liquid rose from the unremarkable
puddle, it formed a robust figure which was
taller and wider than Tecta himself. The
figure still had a fluidity about its form.
    "Do not toy with me shape-shifter," said
Tecta, in a deadly serious tone.
Meld was a partial, elemental shape-shifter.
He could morph between earthly substances such
as rock and fluid. He did not, however, have
the ability to utilise fire or wind. He spat a
globule of thick, gloopy fluid at Tecta's
face. It stuck fast, blinding him momentarily.

Meld took full advantage, he charged at Tecta and transformed his arm into a solid, rocky substance. He swung his oversized boulder of a fist at Tecta. The droid intercepted the attempted blow with his own fist, shattering the boulder on impact.

"Metal beats rock!" he said in a strong, self-assured tone. Tecta thrust both fists into the fluid midriff of the shape-shifter. If his theory was right, his predictable opponent would solidify to trap his arms. Meld was true to form and did exactly as Tecta had expected.

"Are you stuck tin man?" Meld smiled broadly at Tecta, and raised his arms menacingly, like two giant pillars of granite - they were poised to deliver a killer blow to Tecta's head.

"Like I said…" as Tecta spoke he deployed his fist spikes and yanked his arms outward to freedom. Meld's midriff cracked like concrete over a fault line, and his whole torso exploded in a shower of dust and debris "...Metal beats rock."

The debris shimmered as it turned to a fine drizzle that rained gently down onto the arena floor. The drizzle slowly formed numerous puddles across the arena as the liquid welled.

"You clearly weren't paying attention." Tecta detonated a bi-thermic grenade. The liquid that was the warrior Meld froze solid, then suddenly ignited. It rose to such an intense heat that Meld could not regain any form of solidity. He had been reduced to particulates so miniscule that even he could not recover. He became a thin veil of condensation that evaporated into nothing. The crowd went wild, as they cheered and chanted

Tecta's stage name:

"Iron bear! Iron bear!"

"Are you satisfied now?" Tecta shouted up at God, trying to make himself heard over the screams and whooping of the frenzied crowd.

"Mwah!" came Daa'Shond's reply. "This is just an appetiser, an impressive start...but there is so much more to come."

"I was speaking to her, not you."

"God does not converse with the entertainment." A low hiss filled the cavernous space, and it brought with it a deadly hush... the crowd had fallen silent.

"I will speak for myself Daa'Shond."

"Apologies, my lady God," he grovelled in response.

"An impressive warrior you are. However, I find your lack of enthusiasm for the fight concerning. Let me show you something." God clicked her pincers together and a hologram illuminated in the centre of the arena. Tecta saw images of his beloved family and friends, they looked...happy. Maybe he had underestimated their capacity to cope and survive in his absence. He was filled with an overwhelming sense of pride, mildly tainted by the faintest feelings of sadness.

"You see?" God hissed. "They are not merely surviving; they are thriving without you and your extreme methods. What was the last one? That's it, an act of genocide on the planet Feer'aal. A most heinous crime, yet very effective." Tecta hung his head in shame. "Now allow me to show you their alternative existence, should you decide not to fight for me." The hologram grew dark and the scene that was projected before Tecta shook him deep to his core. The Raize lined the perimeter of Unity space. Thousands upon thousands of them, each ready to attack as only The Raize can. "Why would you risk an attack of this magnitude on your children? All you need do is fight for me, and their harmonious existence will continue."

"The Raize? They are an extinct race. I will not fall for your trickery."

"No no! They are not extinct: they are controlled. I thought that might grab your attention."

"How do I know you're not lying? Showing me that which I desire, compared to my most dreaded nightmare."

"Quite simply," she rasped, "You cannot be sure...but are you willing to take that gamble? Will you continue to fight for me? Or will you condemn your precious Unity to death?"

"You underestimate them. However, I do not wish war upon my children. You win...I don't like your game, but I will play."

"If I get the slightest suspicion that you are throwing a fight to orchestrate your own demise... I will order The Raize to attack Unity and give no quarter! Return him to his suite."

"No! I need to know more!"

The arena fell dark and Tecta was escorted back to his 'suite,' although cell was a more apt description of the place they held him.

Chapter Six

Devastation

Tecta's mind raced, full of horror at the mere mention of The Raize. He was relieved to be back in his cell, where he could try to gain some perspective. He was perplexed by how The Raize were still in existence. His mind drifted back to the first time he had heard their name - every detail was crystal- clear. Tecta had stumbled upon a solitary escape pod; it had been adrift, miles from anywhere. The discovery had occurred purely by chance, as no distress signal had been activated to call him there. Tecta beamed the pod aboard his ship, where he discovered a single life form inside. The image of Mimm's face had haunted him for years... that poor creature who had barely lived to tell her tale. The memory of her expression; the picture of pure desperation and hopelessness had faded over time. Now it was back with a vengeance, like an icicle piercing his brain.

"You are safe now," Tecta had said, cradling her in his arms to offer some semblance of security.

"No!" Mimm had said in sheer panic, "None of us are safe."

"You survived," said Tecta.

"I am the only one that did." She broke down again, crying convulsively.

"They were so beautifully majestic, swimming through the skies in graceful waves. We called them The Raize, on account of their startling similarity to the shallow water Winged Ray, that used to be native to the oceans of my home world, before their annihilation. The entire population of the planet had stared skyward in absolute wonder."

"What happened next, dear child?" Tecta asked.

"The end of the world." Mimm barely managed to speak the words.

Tecta held her in an attempt to steady her jolting body as she sobbed. He felt a shift, a sudden calm descend upon Mimm, a kind of voluntary surrender. Everything she knew was gone, including her will to live. She slipped away in his arms. Tecta had never believed that any living being could actually die from a broken heart. Those few brief moments spent with Mimm had convinced him otherwise. Any creature that could inflict this level of fear and helplessness on another living being, needed to be eradicated.

Chapter Seven

The Nothing

The Core Loway came to a grinding halt mid-phase shift, the jump between planetary cores wasn't always smooth, but this sudden jolt was strong enough to send Pilot and Pilot hurtling through the air. The pair landed in a scruffy heap by the forward bulkhead. The interior of the vessel went pitch black.

"Pilot hit head, Pilot no see no things," moaned the croaky-voiced pilot.

"Dis cos light go out dum dum," said Pilot, fumbling to find something to pull himself up on.

"Phew!" the croaky Pilot sighed with relief, "Pilot think Pilot blinded by bang head."

"Pilot, you touch a thing?" Pilot's voice rang out in the dark, accusingly.

"Why Pilot always blame Pilot?" came the croaky reply.

"Because is Pilot fault most time!"

"No true, Pilot the one say, "Pilot no touch, Pilot no touch," then Pilot touch...and BAM! Big problem."

"Pilot hush, you know no things."

"Dis big Loway problem?"

"Pilot not know."

A beam of light pierced the darkness. It swayed from side to side, moving unsteadily towards them.

"Pilot strong, you no mess Pilot!" Pilot shouted at the approaching light. His chest puffed out and fists clenched.

"You Pilot, grab light, Pilot hit," Pilot croaked in a whisper.

"No, *you Pilot* grab light, *Pilot* hit," Pilot snapped in reply. A deep laugh came from the dark ...a thick-fingered hand grabbed the swaying light and angled it downward. It was a miner's lamp, and it was attached to the head of a very rotund Pilot who waddled towards the pair.

"Oh Ha ha, Pilot think funny?" cried the croaky-voiced Pilot.

"Dis no funny." Pilot was extremely unimpressed. He shook his head despairingly. The thick laughter continued.

"What smell? Pilot scare Pilots bad, Pilots do mess? Ha ha ha," the chunky Pilot's laughter continued.

"Dis no funny, Loway no break never." A searing light and a burst of energy passed through the Loway, it made all three Pilots momentarily weightless and disorientated. The Loway was in motion again, but something was wrong, they were travelling in the wrong direction. Pilot jumped to the controls, but course correct was not responding. Something else had taken control of the Core Loway.

"No, no this bad friend Pilots," Pilot's voice wavered audibly.

"What happens Pilot?" asked the croaky-voiced Pilot.

"Loway, go to The Nothing," said Pilot grimly.

"The Nothing? What dis nothing?" asked the robust Pilot.

"The Nothing, Loway dead end," Pilot

answered.

"Loway no slow down, hit nothing. Bad big boom?" asked the round Pilot.

"No pilot ever been to nothing before, Pilot get Raktee."

"Dis bad, Pilot no touch Raktee years," croaked Pilot.

"No! Dis is end, we drink for end, honour all Pilots ever been ever."

For the first time ever, Pilot wished the Loway would slow down. But, whatever was controlling it, clearly had other ideas. The Loway gained more and more momentum with every passing second. Pilot tracked their position on the Loway map. They grew closer and closer to The Nothing.

"We warn other Pilots on Loway?" asked croaky-voiced Pilot.

"No!" was Pilot's reply, "They no need to be scared, this over soon."
The rotund Pilot raised his glass.

"Pilot happy with friends at end."

"Drink to Pilots, may friends be safe."
The three of them downed their drinks and embraced each other fondly. Their journeys end had come: the Loway collided with The Nothing and...

Chapter Eight

Son of Raktar II

Alarms blared in ear-splitting screams and seizure-inducing lights flashed violently, as Taire ran through the claustrophobic corridors of the complex. Clint followed, beeping maniacally.

"Yes, I did say these are my people." Clint trilled aggressively.

"Clearly I was wrong! Stop being a know it all and locate the hanger, we need to get to The Seeker. Our ship is the only way off this planet!" Clint gave a despondent groan.

"It's locked down! Can you detect any other modes of transport?" Taire was disorientated, so much had just happened. He needed some space to try to figure everything out.
Clint bleeped repeatedly.

"Tell me those are happy bleeps?" His frenzied bleeping continued.

"Speeders! That will do just fine." Clint darted ahead, and Taire gave chase, trying his best to keep up. It didn't take him long to reach the Speeder Bay. Taire arrived seconds after Clint, who had already powered up a speeder. He leapt into the pilot seat and engaged thrusters. The bay doors should've opened automatically as they approached, but they showed no sign of budging.

"Clint, lock onto something... we're

blasting our way out of here."
Taire unleashed a trio of plasma bolts that
cleaved the doors wide open. Clint gave an
elated squeal of celebration.

"Yes, we are free... now we need to stay
that way." Taire engaged maximum thrusters;
the hijacked speeder powered through the
frozen gorges of the Raktarian landscape with
ease. The wind whipped through Taire's hair,
and the freezing blasts of air felt raw
against the exposed skin of his hands and
face. To be outside was a relief, but what he
wouldn't give for his excessively furry, puffy
jacket right now. Clint chirruped.

"Oh! You're cold! You don't even have
nerve endings. I can't feel my fingers or my
face."

There was no time for bickering or
disagreements, the Raktarians were giving
chase. Energy bolts sizzled overhead - their
pursuers clearly didn't want to kill them.
Either that, or they were the worst shots they
had ever encountered. The fire overhead caused
Clint to screech in panic. Taire looked up,
clouds raced across the sky, backlit by the
brilliant blue light of the new moon which
exaggerated their velocity. The pace of the
speeder exaggerated it even further. He needed
to focus.

"Clint, calm down and scan the area, find
us some cover." Clint gave a series of squeaks
and trilling sounds.

"Are you sure? That's insane," Taire
responded.

"Blruup." Clint gave an angry grunt.

"Okay, of course I trust you."

Clint had told Taire to head directly into,

what at first glance, looked like a solid rock face. Taire linked navigation controls to Clint's systems. Taire's wits, as well as his hands, were frozen. He didn't have the wherewithal or dexterity to perform the intricate manoeuvres required to navigate the narrow path Clint had mapped out. The Raktarian speeders had stopped firing at them. Taire took a look behind them and instantly saw why. One of the speeders had gained on them, and the pilot was weaving left and right, trying to get alongside them. Taire knew what was coming next: the tried and tested side-swipe manoeuvre, but he had a trick up his sleeve, (an oldie but a goodie). Ahead of them the mountain pass forked: this could be the prime opportunity...

"Clint, ease off the throttle and hold on tight." The Raktarian pilot eased up alongside them and Taire hit the power switch, which stalled the speeder. The Raktarian shot ahead and darted into the left fork in the path. Taire instantly restarted the speeder - the other Raktarians couldn't be far behind.

"Clint go right," shouted Taire. Clint veered hard to the right and entered a treacherous passage. He skillfully negotiated the rocky outcrops of the narrow path. The Raktarian speeders entered through the fork behind them.

Ahead was a sheer rock face, and they were headed for it at a breakneck pace. If they made it through what Taire hoped was a sophisticated optical illusion, Clint would then have to navigate the mess of tunnels that lay beyond. Taire squeezed his eyes tightly shut.

"I hope you're right friend," he shouted,

and the speeder disappeared into the rock
face.
The Raktarians who had given chase, screamed
to a halt just shy of the spot where Taire's
speeder had vanished. Nevis, the lead speeder
pilot, screamed something indecipherable
through gritted teeth, and pounded his fist
against his speeder's console, inadvertently
activating the vehicles comms.

"Son Nevis, report," came Reynar's voice
through the comm-link. "I said report! Have
you secured them?" Reynar's words were filled
with impatience and frustration as they
blasted from the comms. Nevis was caught off-
guard. He sighed heavily, then cleared his
throat before he gave his nervy reply.

"Negative Son Reynar, they have entered
The Wilds."

"Well! You are supposed to be a skilled
pilot. If you are not equipped to navigate The
Wilds on your vehicles, then you will have to
track them on foot."

"But, entering The Wilds, it is forbidden
by the word of the Dark Mother herself."

"Well, *I* forbid you to let them get away!!
Am I making myself understood?"

"Yes, Son Reynar." Nevis gestured to the
other speeder pilots to dismount and follow
him.

"But, Son Nevis, it's The Wilds," said
Sanvar, the youngest member of the group.

"I'm fully aware of that, but you heard
Son Reynar's order. We have no choice, let's
go."

"Dark Mother, may you forgive us this
treacherous act."
Sanvar looked skyward and offered a fleeting
plea for forgiveness, then reluctantly
followed the other speeder pilots through the

gateway to The Wilds.

The twist and swerve of the speeder was
nausea-inducing as Clint negotiated the
tightly-winding tunnels. Taire felt grateful
that his stomach was empty. Clint squealed in
panic - the tunnels were about to get too
tight for even him to find safe passage
through. Without a second to spare, Taire
grabbed hold of Clint and threw them both
clear of the doomed speeder, which slammed
into the cave wall. He thumped down hard on
the ground and rolled clear of the exploding
wreckage. The speeder had spectacularly lost
its face-off with the cavern wall. The impact
with the solid ground forced the air sharply
from Taire's lungs. He lay flat-out on the
floor, in a bid to regain his breath.
    "Clint," Taire gasped, "Are you okay?"
Clint had been flung from his grip during the
fall. No reply came back.

    "I know who you are, and why you have come
here." A thick, warm voice filled the
darkness. It was the same voice Taire had
heard behind the door of the Archive Room,
which itself now seemed like an age ago.
    "Who's there? Show yourself!" coughed
Taire, gasping for breath. He tried to peer
through the veil of dust and smoke that the
collision had created.
    "Now, now, I expect better manners from my
guests, especially from a child of The Unity."
The owner of the velvety voice stepped out of
the darkness into view. He was an old man,

dressed in simple, loose-fitting, cotton clothes. His features were weathered, sage-like, and his bright glistening eyes carried an uncommon wisdom. Suddenly, the sound of Clint's best attempt at a battle cry, squealed from the darkness. It was accompanied by the small roar of his micro boosters igniting. He flew from the shadows and headed straight at the old man.

"Clint, no!" shouted Taire, He was too late to stop the little droid's attack. The old man dodged Clint's attempted assault with ease, and the droid clattered into the wall, trilling and beeping in confusion.

"Please excuse my friend. Clint, get over here!" The old man waved his hand dismissively, and Clint sheepishly floated over to Taire.

"How do you know me?" asked Taire, his tone was laced with suspicion.

"Unless I am very much mistaken, you are the Pure One... the unblemished son of Raktar. You have returned to cleanse us all of the darkness we have wrought in our misguided past, to lead Raktar once more into the light."

"Well, not exactly - not at all in fact. I came here for knowledge, to learn of my heritage and find out who I really am."

"Follow me," said the strange old man. He led them through a dimly-lit network of tunnels. The place was reminiscent of The Silence back on Unity, with the same type of luminous rocks guiding their way. They came to a clearing, which was lit by a glowing red gem embedded within the ground.

"Please sit," the old man gestured to the bare ground, where a seat of sorts, in the form of a short pillar of stone, rose from the cave floor. "You are the Pure One, what more would you need to know? You certainly are not a seeker or a fanatical, hmmm." The old man teased the tip of his beard between his forefinger and thumb. "Maybe you've been corrupted by too much sunlight. You are very tanned for a Raktarian; sunlight and us Raktarians are not a good mix, you know. We are the outermost planet of our solar system."

"No, I don't know. That's the whole point of me being here. I don't know anything of Raktar, except the weapons we've faced, such as the Shrapnel Droids and the A.R.K's"

"Please Pure One, don't speak of our people's shame. The guilt is too much to bear."

"You were being influenced by The Hushed, you couldn't help your actions, and please could you call me Taire?"

"Very kind of you to say so, Taire. But, some of us could, and should have, kept ourselves in check during those darkest of times."

"What do you mean by that?"

"The Fanaticals," he whispered. "The extremist engineers - they were just waiting for the opportunity to push things too far, in the name of 'science'. They performed forbidden procedures, unspeakable acts, and modifications on sentient droid species. It is unfortunate that they got to you first. You must believe me when I tell you that they are not what Raktar stands for. They were too easily turned; they deny our true heritage and choose to continue in their efforts to resurrect 'the Mother,' or the 'Dark Mother', to reveal her true name."

"The Dark Mother?"

"We have nothing to hide here." Clint played back the words Reynar had spoken earlier.

"Thanks for your valuable input Clint," Taire tutted.

"Don't dismiss your small friend so readily. He is far more aware than he first seems, and he is right. They are hiding a great deal. Not least of all their pursuit of the Dark Mother. She is a creature from our galaxy's dark past that the Fanaticals have chosen to make their God. For scientists, they are uncommonly superstitious and easily led. The Elders never wanted the truth of who we Raktarians really are to be revealed. Our planet contains the most valuable, precious metals in the galaxy. We were meant to use these resources to further the advancement of all the people of the galaxy. But, the Elders became possessive, consumed by greed and the desire to use these metals for their own gain. The introduction of the Dark Mother was a convenient method of keeping the new generations in line, and it stuck. Even The Hushed used the Fanatical's belief in the Dark Mother; they swayed them to create vile weapons in her name, many of which you have witnessed the horrors of. Those weapons were forged using the suffering and stolen technology of other species. Nel was one such tragedy, but now we can rectify their mistakes. She is to be an integral part of your next journey."

"What's a Nel?"

"Nel was an extraordinary specimen... the legacy of a long-lost technologically advanced species. Nel came in peace to seek asylum among our people, thinking us to be like-

minded scientists. A lone being who just
wanted somewhere to belong."
His eyes welled with tears and grew distant,
calling upon memories from a time long past.

"What a feat of engineering excellence. A
sentient droid with deployable and retrievable
component parts. Those component parts could
perform tasks independently of the whole, and
each component was intelligent and aware. The
Fanaticals ignored that brilliance, and
instead saw an opportunity to create a
devastating weapon. They disabled Nel and
dissected her systems, completely
disassembling every relay and scrap of tech to
create the Shrapnel Droids. That, however, was
not the cause of her demise. When Nel was
reassembled, her system went into full
defensive mode. She quite rightly obliterated
her Raktarian captors. But Nel couldn't live
with that; she was empathetic, acutely aware
of the feelings of others, so she went into
total shut down after the incident, appalled
by what she had done. She has slept ever
since." The old man looked heartbroken. "I
took the liberty of embedding a complete set
of the Raktarian archives into Nel's system,
then I brought her here, where we have
remained. You, the Pure One, can create
sentient life forms. Look at your little
friend here - he's a perfect example. There
has not been a Pure One since he who woke the
Protector Droids in the Dawn Wars. You Taire,
have the power to wake Nel."

"So, how long have you been living here,
alone?" Taire's tone was wary, thinking the
old man may have gone insane in his isolation.

"I have always been here or hereabouts.
I've been waiting."

"Waiting for what exactly?"

"For you Taire. I refused to believe that the traitors of the core territories are all that remained of our people. They procrastinate, laying upon their bed of lies, denying what has happened here...and what they've become. I have instead dwelled amongst these caves, forging the data key to unlock The First's knowledge."

"You know of The First?"

"I do, but before we get to that, tell me something Taire. In the days and years since the Unity Spire was activated, have you had any contact from Raktar? Communication of any kind? Offers of assistance in times of war or hardship? Perhaps a congratulations, or even an extended hand in friendship even?"

"No, nothing."

"Do you not think that is odd? When one of our own people, such as you Taire, has played a most significant role in saving the galaxy not once, but twice. First from The Hushed, and then Injis?"

"I assumed that it was due to misplaced shame for acts carried out in the name of The Hushed, that the people couldn't forgive themselves." The old man's eyes widened.

"NO! You think that way because you are the Pure One, and you try to see the best in others. You take for granted that others think as you do. They are not pure. They revel in that which should bring them shame. They take pride in their monstrous creations; they bide their time, waiting for the Dark Mother to return, so that they may take her side when she attempts to rule all. We will make no excuses for them." For a brief moment, the old man was completely enraged.

"You are the truest Raktarian on this planet: unblemished and uncorrupted. You will be the saviour of Raktar. Now, you must leave this place... before their dark temptation blackens your pure heart."

"But, I came here for answers."

"All the answers you need are inside Nel, but you will need to revive her to access the archives." He handed Taire a pristine key.

"What is it?"

"A key."

"I can see that, but a key to what?"

"It will unlock the knowledge of The First, and so much more. Now you must take Nel and go: fulfil your destiny Pure One." He pointed, and Taire's eyes followed the gesture. A droid like none he'd ever seen before had appeared, slumped in the shadows, like a metallic ragdoll.

"But who are you?"

"I am Raktar."

"How?" was Taire's stunned response. The old man smiled warmly.

"As you and your siblings commune with the planet Unity through the Spire, I commune with you through these caves - albeit in a more traditional sense." He paused and tilted his head to one side, as if listening to a distant sound.

"Fanaticals are approaching. This place may soften the dark grip that has ensnared some of them, but not all. They could be the seed that begins to bring our people back to who we were meant to be. Mind what you tell them, as some are beyond redemption. Make allies of those that you can, and bring them back to the light. Restore our people's legacy."

"I don't understand how."

"Awaken Nel, ...and Taire, take these... they will help." Two flat metallic rings lay on the ground before Taire.

"What are they?"

"The O blades. Ve'dow, (defence), and Ki'resh, (attack). The traditional weapon of our people. Take them. You are a worthy beneficiary of the long-forgotten craftsmanship that forged them."

"I'm no warrior. Lu and Gliis are the warriors."

"That is why I give you this gift. Raktarian's are not natural combatants. These will give you an edge. Use them in conjunction with your feelings and intellect, and always utilise your surroundings."

"What do they do?"

"So many questions. Take the blades and let them lead you. Now go, may The Unity guide you, for peace."

Taire stooped to pick up the rings - they were deceptively light, and glowed in response to his touch. The two shimmering circles emitted a powerful energy. Taire stood up, regarding the strange weapons he had been given. When he eventually looked up, the old man was gone.

Chapter Nine

The Link In The Silence

Kee'Pah was roused from her slumber by Gliis' restlessness. He tossed and turned in his sleep, and beads of cold sweat ran down his clammy skin.

"Child of Raktar, you must fulfil your birthright. You must find and wake me, your one true god." Gliis's eyes snapped open, the chilling voice lingered in his mind.

"Bad dream?" asked Kee'Pah, as she evaporated the sweat away from Gliis' face with gentle licks of blue fire that danced at her fingertips.

"No, I fear this is much worse. Taire is in grave danger. We must consult The Silence."

Gliis and Kee'Pah had devoted the last five years to studying the sentient planets together, in an attempt to gain some understanding of why they had fallen silent, (with the exception of the Unity Spire), and the recently awakened Veela VI and Mora. They had so far only had one success; they had found a pocket of The Link deep within The Silence. They had learned that The Link was once an entity so enormous that it spanned what were now the Core Loway routes. The Link connected the sentient planets to one another, enabling them to act as a cohesive community. The Link was the primary means of

communication between the sentient worlds.
This was, (by their own admission), a very
significant find, but they continued to strive
to learn more. Gliis had a special fondness
for The Link; they had made his first meeting
possible with his mother, Etala Maas, and had
also enabled him to communicate with his now
beloved Kee'Pah, (when her essence was in
limbo, trapped within the subterranean aqua-
gel sea on Mora). Gliis thought of the last
time Etala had appeared to him. It was in a
dream, and she had said;

    "To survive the future, you must first
understand the past." Deep down he somehow
knew that this would be the last time his
mother would appear to him, in dream or
spectral form. He, and the other Children of
The Unity, had been handed the torch to carry
the light into their future.

                    * * * * * * * * * *

Gliis and Kee'Pah knew almost every nook and
cranny of The Silence, unless the gems were
feeling particularly playful and turned their
usual trick of re-shaping the walls, to cause
confusion. The caves always returned to their
original shape after the gems had had their
fun. Gliis and Kee'Pah had spent many hours,
days, weeks and even months at a time down
here. The gems embedded in the cavern's walls
lit in recognition, welcoming the pair's
presence. The jewels glowed and pulsed,
lighting the way to The Link that lay deeper
within. Kee'Pah loved to trail her fingers
along the wall as they walked, causing a
rippling light show in response from the gems.

It was this purity and innocence that had
always attracted Gliis to Kee'Pah. She
embodied a natural, soothing calm and a
boundless sense of fun and wonder. The two of
them were viewed as the people's sweethearts;
the bright young things, and in the hearts and
minds of the citizens of the New Unity - they
were the key to the future.
The Silence felt different today. There was an
almost imperceptible, electric buzz about the
caves. No sooner had the pair reached The Link
in The Silence, The Link illuminated, and
there before them stood Taire. He wielded a
strange weapon - bright beams of laser light
and streaks of molten fire lit up the scene.
He appeared to be in a cave very similar to
the ones Gliis and Kee'Pah had just passed
through.

"Taire!" shouted Gliis, but his brother
couldn't hear him. The events that The Link
was showing them were happening elsewhere in
The Unity.

"Can you feel that?" Kee'Pah asked Gliis.
At this moment he was too emotionally invested
in his brother to sense anything else.

"No, what is it?"

"I sense a darkness, a presence in that
cave, like white noise. It's focused around
Taire."

"We need to go," said Gliis, "We need to
tell Lu."

"Wait." A strange whisper of a voice, warm
and intoxicating, rooted them to the spot.

"You must hear us." A dense, dry mist rose
like an all-encompassing wall. It wasn't
threatening in anyway, in fact it was calming,
serene even. Several oddly-shaped silhouettes
shifted within the mist.

"Who are you?" asked Gliis.

"Look inside yourselves, you both already know the answer to that question."

"Are you Unity?" asked Gliis.

"We speak as the sentient worlds of the galaxy. We need you to understand..."

"Understand what exactly?" Kee'Pah queried.

"Why we became dormant and more importantly, why we are waking up again. We were battered into submission by the relentless bombardment and catastrophic ravages of war. The people of our individual planets were incapable of working together to defend the galaxy. If they wouldn't come together to defend themselves, then why should we continue to endure this punishment? when it was us who had given them life. We took decisive action and severed The Link that bound us to one another. The caves of Raktar fell silent, and the Eye of Veela receded into the planet's surface. The Link itself was not only severed, but scattered throughout the farthest reaches of our galaxy. Unity hosted the statement that we had decided upon making - we created the Liberty and Crest Spikes. As you now know from experience, when these two artefacts are connected, the result is the Unity Spire. We, the planets, vowed to never reawaken until the people had proved themselves worthy heirs to our worlds, by coming together to activate the Unity Spire. We did not take this decision lightly, and it affected us deeply. However, the greater goal is more important than our own discomfort, or the crushing isolation we had subjected ourselves too."

"The Royals never achieved such a union during their reign, nor did they even question

why we had, in their eyes, abandoned them.
Instead, they renamed us as the Sovereign
Planets, believing that our sentience was lost
forever. Despite the good that the Royals
tried to do, and the peace they presided over,
the people of the galaxy were still painfully
separate. It wasn't until more recent times,
(when Gerrin Flax had been chosen to take the
mantle of King of the House of Royals, and
made public his forbidden relationship with
Etala Maas), that anyone had even thought such
a union could be a possibility. Their
relationship is what gave rise to the plan to
unite the galaxies - for people as equals to
take us forward, into a new age. We watched in
hope as children were chosen from each of the
'sovereign worlds' to be raised and trained by
the Royal Protector Droids. The droids
understand to this day, the importance of
peace and tolerance. They had been privy to
the secret knowledge of the Core Loway: the
means to pass quickly from one planet to
another. The Loway was built to follow the
routes inhabited by The Link. In the time
since The Link had been disconnected, the
Loway had been used to mine us safely close to
our core, since we had imposed our 'sleep'. We
stopped gifting our precious metals, minerals,
water and energy to the surface by natural
means. Tecta and Etala gifted the Loway to the
care of Pilots. These seemingly unassuming
creatures understood the value of caring for
the planets - since their own world was so
barbarically stripped by Scavengers - who took
every last scrap of her life-giving elements.
The efforts of all concerned were in vain. The
Feruccians and Slaavene, spurred on by The
Hushed and armed with the vicious weapons that
the Raktarians had created, shattered the

dream of united peace. We had lost all hope until now."

   "We have responded to your progress - you have learnt and grown, yet there is still much to do. But, we are willing to help. You have made a bold start. Activating the Unity Spire was your first leap towards understanding. You have earned the respect of Veela VI and Mora, by bringing about their resurrection. They, in turn, used the remnants of The Link to bring about which we had already observed, to our attention. Even Raktar, the planet we feared forever lost to us, has communicated with your brother Taire. Here, in The Silence of Unity - you have helped your cause greatly. You have proven your willingness and hunger to learn. Until all the pieces are in place, the galaxy remains vulnerable...."

Gliis and Kee'Pah were wrapt in the story of the sentient planets, and had sat respectfully, listening to every word.
   "We are honoured, and we thank you for sharing your history with us. We will continue to learn and grow," said Gliis.
   "We give thanks for your help. We must succeed where those before us have failed," added Kee'Pah.
   "Go now, preparations must be made. For peace." The mist receded as swiftly as it had arrived. Gliis and Kee'Pah leapt to their feet and ran. Time was of the essence....

Chapter Ten

Son of Raktar III

"Son Ko'tou, Son Sanvar, this way," commanded Nevis, "Turn off your beams, let the light of the catacombs guide you." Sanvar had always been afraid of the dark, well... afraid of everything would be a more apt description. He was possibly the most irrational and superstitious Raktarian in the planet's history. Joining the militia had been his parent's idea. *It will toughen you up,* they had told him. Nurture had never been their strength. Still, Sanvar had done well, and had held his own in the corps. But this... this sacrilege, and wilful abandon of the Mother's teachings, was too much. It all felt like a horrendous mistake that would end very badly.

"Son Sanvar, come on," grunted Ko'Tou.
"Okay, coming," said Sanvar, as he fumbled to turn off his beam and immediately felt the panic rise within him. *"Breathe,"* he said to himself, *"Just breathe."* The rest of the party had pushed on, and he scurried, feeling his way along the jagged walls to catch them. A deafening blast, and flashes of light, went off ahead of him.

"Son Ko'Tou, Son Nevis, are you okay?" He shouted into the darkness ahead.

"Stop asking questions and get in here, we need back up now." Sanvar hurried towards the

voices. Ko'Tou and Nevis were concealing
themselves in the shadowy crevices of the
caves. Sanvar followed suit, nestling himself
in a tight crook in the cave wall.

"Where are the others?" he asked.

"They went on ahead, and judging by the
sounds we just heard, they won't be coming
back out," answered Ko'Tou.

"Hush!" grunted Nevis, "We need to out-
think this enemy: he is no fool. He has killed
some of our best men. We must make him pay."

"But Son Nevis, Son Reynar said he needs
him alive," said Sanvar.

"To hell with Reynar! We need to take the
enemy out. It's him or us, and I'm not ready
to die just yet. Are you with me?"

"I am, let's get this done," said Ko'Tou.
Sanvar gulped, he could only muster the word
"Yes," albeit very unconvincingly.

"Okay, Ko'Tou you go left, I'll go right.
Sanvar - once we've engaged him you advance -
and end him with the liquidator canon. I'm
trusting you with this. Do not let me down."

"Okay," Sanvar replied, his voice
trembling.

Nevis gave the silent command to attack. Like
a predatory Ka'at, he clawed at the air. He
and Ko'Tou charged from their hiding places,
weapons drawn and primed to fire. Sanvar
stepped out from the shadows and prepared to
follow them into the fray. The cave started to
vibrate violently. Green beams of crackling
light pierced the darkness, and they drew
intricate lines all about the cave. It was
mesmerising... Then... a lethal metal ring
whirred out of the darkness and hovered in the
air ominously. The ring spun, gaining
momentum, and it transformed into a pinwheel

of molten metal, bursting forward with a high-pitched whine. The wheel of fire powered along the lines that the beams had previously drawn, spinning furiously as it carved its way along the etched green lines, like a monorail on a track. Sparks flew, and the dizzying circle of fire left precisely gouged trails of molten rock in its wake, where huge chunks of stone were carved from the walls and ceiling of the cave. The boulders crashed down, trapping Nevis and Ko'Tou beneath their considerable bulk. Sanvar stepped cautiously towards his fallen brothers in arms.

"End him!" came the shout from Nevis, "Avenge your brothers."
Taire stood in the clearing before Sanvar, clutching O blades that glowed with a crackling green fire.
"There is no need for you to get hurt," said Taire sincerely, "I am here to bring Raktar back to its rightful standing in the galaxy. You have been lied to by your people."
"End him now!" screamed Nevis, but Sanvar was rooted to the spot.
"I don't want to hurt you, and I don't believe that you want to hurt me, as you haven't even raised your weapon."
"Coward! Kill him!" screamed Nevis.
"No," said Sanvar, in an assured, level tone. "I will not."
"Then it's treason. When Son Reynar hears of this, you will be hunted down and shown no mercy." Clint hovered over to where Nevis lay, and tasered him in the face with a static charge. He was out cold.
"Did the Mother send you?" Sanvar asked Taire.
"No, I am Taire of the New Unity. What is

your name?"

"I am Sanvar."

"I know you don't know me, but I need you to trust me."

"I know that you are a hero of the galactic conflicts, and that you are a son of Raktar."

"I can clearly see that you are not like your colleagues here." He gestured to the piles of rock that restrained Nevis and the now deceased Ko'Tou. "They took the first opportunity to try to kill me. No questions, no chance to surrender. They meant to murder me without hesitation."

"You're right. I am not like them. I have never found out where I fit in, and they ridiculed me for it. I took solace in the stories of the Mother, because it is said that she will lead us forward." The caves had indeed softened Sanvar's beliefs.

"I will be honest with you Sanvar - I know nothing of the Mother. I have, however, seen many things that most people would believe to be impossible. I sensed that something was very wrong here. Raktar itself has confirmed this and asked me for help."

"What?... Are you some kind of planet whisperer?"

"No," laughed Taire, "But I do have the ability to commune with the sentient planets, as do my brother and sister. Raktar has given me these ancient O blades, along with this droid..." He pointed towards Nel's lifeless body. "And a crucially important mission. I need to put this all together to restore Raktar. I cannot do this alone. Will you help me Sanvar?" The two stood dead still - regarding each other.

Clint shattered the silence with an ear-splitting squeal. Nevis had regained consciousness, and had his blaster levelled at Taire. A red-hot energy bolt blasted from the weapon, followed swiftly by a thoomping sound as Sanvar liquidated Nevis. Taire used the Ve'dow ring to deflect Nevis's shot out of harms way. Sanvar's face drained of all colour.

"Clearly my instincts favour your cause over theirs," he said, trying unsuccessfully to hold in the wave of vomit that rose in his throat. He gagged and wretched, and a fountain of sour fluid spewed out of his gaping mouth onto the cave floor.

"That was your first kill wasn't it?" Taire asked. He placed a comforting hand on Sanvar's back.

"Yes," he replied, straightening up and wiping his mouth and chin with the back of his hand.

"If it's any consolation, his death was inevitable. The injuries from the rock fall were already too severe to heal."

"I guess I just made myself public enemy number one," he replied, as he spat out the last of the vomit.

"Not at all. You just took a huge step towards a better future."

"Nevis was right about one thing. Once Reynar discovers a Raktarian weapon killed Nevis, and they realise all the bodies are accounted for except mine, he will put two and two together. I will be hunted relentlessly."

"Our mission is far more important than any one person's vendetta against you. In time, everyone will see that, and what has happened here today will take on a whole new complexion. The new Unity will protect and welcome you as one of their own."

"I guess there's no turning back now," said Sanvar, managing a nervous smile, "What happens next Taire?"

"Blunkt," groaned Clint.

"What did he say?" Sanvar enquired.

"He asked how we are going to get our ship back, and it's a good question."

"Well, do you have a plan?"

"I do have a great plan... but..."

"I'm not going to like this am I?" said Sanvar, grimly.

"Possibly not, but it will one hundred percent work."

"Okay, what do we need to do?"

Chapter Eleven

Betrayal?

Sanvar's mind raced as he tore through the bitterly cold blizzard. Was he really about to betray everyone and everything he'd ever known, and trust someone he'd only just met? He imagined speeding through the darkness, and the streaking of the snow must have resembled travelling through space at hyper speed. His imaginings momentarily took his mind off the myriad of ways that this could all go horribly wrong. He had never actually left Raktar, but that was all about to change if he could pull this off - and that definitely felt worth the risk.

As the gateway to the core territories came into view, Sanvar's heart was beating so hard it felt fit to burst from his chest. He could see the fearsome silhouette of Reynar against the light of the Speeder Bay. '*I can do this*' he thought. In truth, he had no other choice. He had to make Taire's plan work. He halted his speeder, dismounted, and approached the furious-looking Reynar.

"Why have you returned empty handed? Where are the others?" growled Reynar.

"They are still searching The Wilds, Son Reynar."

"Why in Feer'aal is Son Nevis not

responding to my hails?"

"Forgive him Son Reynar. The Wilds are a dead zone for comms. I have returned to inform you that we have them trapped in The Wilds, and it is just a matter of time until they are captured. Son Nevis needs more charges, energy cells and supplies. He said it could be a long night."

"How is this possible? They are one man and a tiny tin can."

"He is highly-skilled, Son Reynar, and the droid's 'tiny' stature hides the nature of its true ability."

"I have heard enough of Son Nevis' excuses. I will go to The Wilds and capture them myself!"

"Son Reynar, you need not concern yourself with this. Son Nevis has the situation under control."

"He has it about as under control as his drinking and philandering. I will go to them now. Gather what you need, then re-join us in The Wilds. I will give you all a lesson in capture."

"Apologies Son Reynar, as you wish." Reynar mounted his speeder, threw his heavy cloak about his shoulders, and pulled back hard on the throttle. Two further speeders joined him, and they charged into the blizzard that raged beyond the ruined doors of the bay."

Sanvar had managed to hold it together so far, although he was now in a state of panic. As soon as they were out of sight and earshot of the bay security drones, he opened the supply bag that was slung over his shoulder, and Clint hovered out.

"This wasn't part of the plan," he said

frantically. Clint made a clunky groaning sound. "We need to get to your ship and get back to The Wilds before they do, we have to warn Taire." Sanvar ran towards the Hangar as fast as his trembling legs would allow. Clint pushed on ahead. If the Hangar was still locked down, then he had some hacking to do.

* * * * * * * * * *

Reynar and his cohorts blazed through the wretched snow storm, powering through the inhospitable landscape. The entrance to The Wilds was dead ahead. All three speeders launched Thump Charge Missiles. Reynar didn't have the time or patience for the intricacies of navigating the tightly-woven tunnels beyond the rock face. They followed up the missile assault with wave after wave of devastating blaster fire. The entrance to The Wilds was cleaved wide open, and there was now a gaping hole where the tunnels had been just seconds before.

Taire was engrossed in examining Nel when the first volley of missile impacts rocked the cave. The boom echoed through the cavernous space. It sounded like the world was ending. Whatever had caused the cataclysmic noise was unlikely to be friendly. He needed to get Nel out of harm's way or their mission would be over before it had even begun. The only option was to venture deeper into the caves. Taire fashioned a makeshift harness from the strapping of his kit bag and lashed Nel to his back. She was constructed of lightweight alloys, carrying her still involved a fair amount of effort. He moved clumsily through the weaving caves, using the walls and rocky structures of the environment to steady himself. This was not an ideal course of action. *Think Taire think* Then it struck him... *the rings.* He unfastened the loop on which he had used to secure the rings to his belt and held them out in front of him. He inhaled deeply and the rings began to glow. Taire closed his eyes and visualised what he wanted the rings to do. Beams of green light energy surged from Ve'dow, and the beams traced the lines Taire had willed onto the rock. He drew his arms back and launched Ve'dow and Ki'resh... the attack ring carved through the rock like it was softened butter, further and further it bored, slicing through layer upon layer of ancient stone. Taire had willed the rings to create an exit, a path to open air, and they had obeyed. He followed the green light and molten fire-glow of the rings ripping through the rock. He had completely lost all sense of time, it felt like there had only ever been the caves, the molten fire and the weight of Nel on his back. A whistling sounded and a freezing draft invaded his face. Taire never thought he could be so glad to feel bitterly cold air. Snow billowed into the cave - the rings had created the exit he so desperately needed. The opening in the coarse rock came into view - the last few metres were hard work. The tunnel was at a horrible incline, the kind that looks slight but actually saps the energy from your legs. This would've been so much easier if he had equipped his combat suit. A few anti-grav bursts and he would've been out of this mess. He had been naive and left the suit onboard The Seeker, despite Clint's warnings. "*I come in peace,*" had been his self-assured words. He really hoped that Clint and Sanvar were okay, and that they had been successful in their mission. They needed a lucky break about now. Taire reached the opening in the rock, and the rings whirred through the air to return to his grasp.

Taire un-lashed Nel from his back and eased her lifeless body through the opening in the rock. He pushed her clear, then heaved himself up through the snug gap. He found himself on a large plateau; the harsh wind whipped the snow about him. He needed to hide Nel. It made sense that if someone had gone to the effort of bombing the caves, then they must be pretty desperate to find him. It had to be Reynar, and he wasn't likely to be alone. Taire scooped Nel up in his arms and hurried to the edge of the plateau. He peered over the precipice, all that lay below was thick, drifting snow. It wasn't ideal, but it would have to do. He lay flat on his stomach, lowered Nel over the edge, and released her into the blanket of white below, where she vanished from his sight. He set himself to jump down and join her, but it was too late.

"Taire!" Reynar's voice was muffled by the blizzard, but not even the raging elements could disguise the anger that fuelled his scream. Taire turned to face him.

"You were my guest. We extended nothing but kindness and a warm welcome to you. In return, you have wrecked my speeder bay and killed my men. Why?" Reynar was incensed.

"You know only too well why I have done this."

"No I don't. Do you care to enlighten me?"

"Anyone who says *We have nothing to hide here* as many times as you, is clearly hiding something."

"Please, do tell me what big secret you have discovered here."

"The caves have told me all I need to know about you and your fellow Fanaticals."

"Oh I see, the caves have spoken to you. You do realise you sound like a complete lunatic?"

"I can prove that I speak the truth." Taire removed the rings from his belt and held them across his chest like a shield. They glowed and pulsed with planetary energy.

"How is this possible?" raged Reynar. "The rings were lost forever."

"That may have been so, but Raktar has gifted them to me, and has also revealed the secrets of your twisted beliefs."

"Why you? I am a true Son of Raktar. They should be mine, and I mean to take them from you." Taire had been stalling for time. He needed The Seeker to arrive right about now, but there was still no sign of Clint or Sanvar. He was going to have to fight. His combat suit would've come in really handy at this moment.

Reynar's two heavy-set guards emerged from the gap in the plateau. They looked brutal and formidable in their heavy matt-black armour, each of them equipped with a personal arsenal of weaponry.

"Retrieve the O blades now! By any means necessary," bellowed Reynar. The guards drew their side arms and opened fire. Taire had no other choice: he had to put his trust in the rings. He used Ve'dow to create an energy shield. He then launched Ki'resh and proceeded to command it with his sheer will. The ring swerved through the air, making a whining, zinging noise as it sliced through the barrels of his assailant's blasters. Taire used Ve'dow to etch, (the now familiar), green energy lines onto the surface of the plateau. Ki'resh traced along the lines, bringing the molten fire once again. Thanks to the O blades, he had outwitted the guards. The ground where they stood disappeared from under their feet, carved away in a perfect circle. Both guards vanished into the surface of the plateau, as if twin trap doors had opened up and swallowed them whole.

"So Taire, it looks like it's just us." Reynar drew his sword and dagger hilts from beneath his thick cloak, both of which ignited with vicious energy blades. They were raw, spiteful weapons. "I say we do this the old way. A fair fight, one -on -one, no trickery."
   "I'm sure you would love that... now that you've lost your advantage. Why shouldn't I just cut you down with these rings?"
   "That wouldn't be fitting behaviour from the Pure One, a child of The Unity, who strives for peace."
   "Do you honestly think I'm that stupid, or egotistical enough, to fall for a transparent ploy like that?" Taire knew only too well that he was not a gifted fighter, going toe-to-toe with Reynar would be a disastrous move. The mission was more important than his pride, and to do anything less than what was necessary in this moment, would make his view of Tecta's actions a total hypocrisy. He would do what was required to protect the New Unity. Reynar raised his blades and ran at Taire, who in response, launched Ki'resh towards Reynar. It whistled and swerved, then swiftly relieved Reynar of his left foot, as he slammed hard onto the solid rock floor - screaming in

blood-curdling pain.

"Let us go on our way, and I will leave you with your life."

"Us? I see only you. A lonely coward!" roared Reynar.

"My companions will be here soon."

"Companions? You mean that pathetic droid?"

"And Sanvar. He has seen the truth, he is leaving with us."

"Ha ha haaa," Reynar gave a mocking laugh, "This comes as no surprise. Sanvar is weak, always has been and always will be. You two deserve each other, the traitor and the coward." Reynar reached inside his cloak and drew his blaster.

"Don't do this Reynar, you've already lost this fight, don't lose your life too."

"DARK MOTHER! GUIDE MY HAND!!" screamed Reynar. Taire had unleashed the rings before Reynar had finished his cry. The hand that still gripped his blaster was severed in a flash. The rings continued on their course, carving through the rock around Reynar's stricken body, and like his guards before him, Reynar was gone...devoured into the surface of the plateau. An echoing scream of unintelligible profanities was all that remained of him, as he descended the unnatural well-shaft the rings had forged.

* * * * * * * * *

The familiar throaty hum of The Seeker's engines filled Taire's entire being with a warm glow. His pride and joy, constructed by his own hands, had been returned to him. The magnificent craft was impervious to the violent wind and snow, as it descended

gracefully to touch down on the vast plateau.
The entrance ramp hissed and lowered. Clint
flew out of the entrance before the ramp had
even settled, buzzing and trilling like an
over-excited Keal pup.

"It's good to see you too friend," said
Taire. Sanvar alighted the ship, and his face
was filled with relief.

"You did it!" he exclaimed. "And you're
still in one piece."

"Likewise," said Taire, returning the
compliment.

"Brunptt?" Clint sounded puzzled.

"Nel?" Taire replied, "She is safe, I had
to hide her. We will retrieve her once we're
onboard The Seeker. Come on, I've seen enough
snow to last me a lifetime."

Taire took the lead and boarded The Seeker. He
took the controls. It felt good, like coming
home. He hovered his ship steadily over the
edge of the Plateau and secured maglock on
Nel's body. Taking great care, he guided her
solid but limp body into the loading bay,
where Clint and Sanvar were waiting to receive
her. Clint chirruped to signal that Nel was
onboard and safely stowed. Taire punched in a
set of coordinates, and with a boom of the
engines, they were slicing through the
stratosphere and into open space. Sanvar's
face wore the expression of a child who had
just entered his first sugar floss store.

"Wow!" he slowly exhaled. "It's so vast
and beautiful."

"Savour this moment, as it will become the
norm all too quickly."

"How could anyone ever take this sight for
granted?"

Chapter Twelve

A Big Mistake

"I have something to make you feel more at home, it might even help lift your spirits." Daa'Shond gestured to the doorway. Tecta couldn't believe his eyes; a Pilot entered the room, and walked tentatively towards Daa'Shond. His stumpy, little legs quivered ever so slightly as he went.

"Pilot! Are you okay?" asked Tecta. Pilot blinked sheepishly, "How did you get here?"

"Quite a curious story really," Daa'Shond interrupted, "About one thousand, four hundred and fourty two of your solar rotations ago, I found it floating in Wild Space, in what looked like a bastardized core drill, mwah! But I'm afraid you are missing the point here. Even after what God has shown you today, I believe one can never have too much leverage." Daa'Shond gave a broad grin, exposing his razor-sharp teeth, and patted Pilot on the head condescendingly.

"Let's keep things positive. Think of it as a mascot, a good luck charm if you will, a little reminder of what you are fighting for tomorrow. It's so adorable. Insufferably dim, but such fun. I've actually grown quite fond of it. Sometimes I get so overwhelmed with emotion that I just want to *crush it*."

"Do not hurt him."

"I'm not going to hurt it, that would be barbaric, although I could dispose of it painlessly if you do not comply." He snapped his powerful pincer-like digits together. "Let's see, I could slice it's head off quite painlessly, mwah."

"If you harm him, I *will* kill you."

"Sadly for you, you'll never get the opportunity. Actually, I've always wondered what it would taste like - would consuming it fill my cynical body with some of its clueless joy and innocence?"

"Now I know you are bluffing, it would take more than *that* to make you even barely tolerable."

"Enough posturing. If you refuse to fight for God, you'd be surprised at what I am capable of... in the name of motivation of course. Have you not seen these teeth? Actually it's a shame it can't speak, it has witnessed more than enough to tell you how merciless I can be." Pilot looked at Tecta pleadingly, willing him not to say that Pilots are able to speak. Tecta was on the same page. This could be a great opportunity to gather valuable intel.

"I will leave you two to get acquainted, but don't get too attached." He gnashed his teeth together, flashing a vicious grin, and took his leave.

* * * * * * * * *

"Friend Tecta, him lie. Unity is to be attacked," Pilot spoke as soon as Daa'Shond was out of earshot.

"Tell me what happened, friend Pilot," said Tecta.

"Pilot name Runt now. Hornet out of charge

in Mora battle. Runt think Runt die. *Him* find Runt Wild Space, but him not friend. Him very bad thing."

"It's okay friend Pilot, I mean Runt. May I ask why you have changed your name?"

"Him call Runt. When you hear all time, make stick. Name Runt now."

"You are still a Pilot. I can call you Pilot, if you wish."

"Runt fine, make feel different."

"Do you feel ready to talk now, Runt?" He nodded, then proceeded to tell Tecta how Daa'Shond had kept him as a pet. He had been privy to many secrets, and had valuable information about Antipathy and God's plans. Tecta felt the faint spark of hope smoulder in his belly.

"Tomorrow I must fight again, friend Runt."

"Friend Tecta, must not fight, you face Kaa'Lash. Him big bad."

"I need to fight, or they will grow suspicious. We need to buy ourselves some time to plan our escape, and we need to warn Unity."

"Friend Tecta has plan?"

"I do, but I need your help friend."

"Anything, friend Tecta."

"Does Daa'Shond always take you to the arena?"

"Always, yes."

"Right, I need you to watch him at the fight tomorrow. Look for anything that could use to help us escape."

"Friend Tecta, you strong, you can leave anytime. Make big boom and go."

"Not without you my friend, and not before we've put an end to this hideous rock and its grotesque inhabitants."

Chapter Thirteen

Fight Two

Tecta was escorted to the arena for the second time. Daa'Shond's nasal tones filled the arena once again, stirring up the crowd. Tecta had made a tactical decision to play to the crowd. The more distraction he could create, the more opportunities it gave Runt to investigate. Tecta whipped the gathered masses into a frenzy. He danced around the arena, shadow-boxing like a featherweight fighter, and firing off random bursts from his wrist blasters. A sudden hush descended. Kaa'Lash rolled out menacingly onto the arena, in its usual creepily-slow manner. Tecta launched himself at the closed shell, but he was repelled by the unrelenting surface. He turned the failed attack into a positive, ~~he~~ manoeuvring his body into a backflip, and sold it to the crowd as showboating.

Tecta was in no hurry to confront the horror that dwelled inside the mammoth shell, and there was no point in wasting energy trying to crack it open. He stood statuesque and waited. What seemed like an eternity passed... suddenly, Kaa'Lash let out the familiar screams from its shell vents, signalling its intention to open. The crowd's hush was suddenly broken with a hiss, as the giant

shell eased open. A mess of tentacles erupted
from within and thrashed ferociously through
the air. Tecta took up a defensive stance with
his twin sabres deployed. He painted the
picture of a cyborg samurai who was poised and
ready to strike. Kaa'Lash launched its
powerful limbs at the motionless droid. Tecta
reacted instantaneously; launching himself
high into the air, and performing a twisting
double somersault. As he spun through the air,
he lashed out with his blades. The strikes
were powerful and precisely measured, with
each pass relieving Kaa'Lash of multiple
limbs. Tecta's spirit faltered as the severed
limbs regenerated as quickly as they were cut
down. Tecta had to think fast, it would be
futile to keep slashing at those seemingly
invincible tentacles. Using his boosters, he
held himself motionless above Kaa'Lash, and
allowed himself to be caught by the kracken-
esque limbs. Kaa'Lash's tentacles wrapped
themselves hungrily around Tecta's body. He
was encased in flesh and muscle. He powered up
to full thrust, in an attempt to rise and rip
the tentacles from the fleshy body within the
shell. They stretched, but would not break.
The suffocating droid was dragged down into
Kaa'Lash's shell, and it snapped shut
violently. Tecta was trapped... helpless it
seemed...like an insect inside a carnivorous
plant. With a unified gasp, the crowd, like
the arena itself, fell silent.

Something was amiss. Kaa'Lash had not yet
performed its trademark victory spin. A few
long, motionless moments passed. Kaa'Lash's
shell vents sounded again; the shrill scream
cut through the ears of the masses, setting
every being's teeth on edge, and causing every

eye in the crowd to squint. Kaa'Lash's gargantuan shell shuddered and jolted violently. A deep, gut- wrenching thud sounded - it was akin to a depth charge. Then with a mighty *crack*!!! Kaa'Lash erupted in a spectacular shower of splintered shell, and vile lumps of gore. Once the debris had cleared, all that remained was the figure of Tecta, both arms raised, holding Kaa'Lash's dense black eye aloft. He launched it into the air, and as the eye began its descent, he launched himself up, fists first, ~~up~~ to meet it. Tecta engaged his fist spikes on impact with the eye, where it exploded into millions of vicious shards of violence. The spiteful splinters impaled many of the front row of spectators. This only served to raise the frenzied crowd up to new heights.

Tecta fired plumes of chaff into the air, creating a makeshift pyrotechnic display. He stomped around the arena, playing to the crowd. He wasn't much of an actor, but he had play-acted his way into the affections of the fickle crowd, as well as the onlooking God and Daa'Shond.

"I do believe he's coming around, my lady God."

"This is a most fortuitous turn of events. She who must be served will soon be with us."

"...And when does this glorious being arrive?"

"Oh trust me, you will know when she arrives," God spoke, in a spine-chilling whisper.

Chapter Fourteen

The Creator

Taire put The Seeker into orbit around the small moon of Treygar. The Treygan race was still in its infancy - technologically naive, living a simple life off the land. They would be completely unaware of The Seeker's presence. Taire envied them in some respects, not being an active part of the chaos that had embroiled the rest of the galaxy.

He stood over his starkly-illuminated workstation, and gave a heavy sigh.
    "Am I destined to be surrounded by neurotic, self-loathing AI? First Tecta, and now possibly you." He was talking to Nel's lifeless body as he worked on her systems. "Neither of you have anything to be sorry about. You were violated, and your tech was stolen to create the darkest of weapons. You had every right to defend yourself." A digital chirruping sounded.
    "Yes Clint, I know you don't feel bad about anything...ever. That is equally as annoying, but you are a totally different prospect." Clint trilled gently.
    "No, I'm not saying that you are special." Clint trilled a little more quietly.
    "No, I'm not going to say it."

Sanvar sat quietly, observing Taire's work. He was struggling to find his space legs, and was feeling less than his best. The wonder of space travel had deteriorated into a gargantuan effort to keep the contents of his stomach down.

Taire looked down at Nel, whom, much to his surprise, was awake, and looking back at him quizzically. Her face lit up with a brilliant smile. She laughed... it was a joyous, metallic sound.

    "Hello handsome, who are you?"
Taire was about to answer when Nel pressed her finger to his lips, "Shhhh, I think I already know." She smiled softly, "Actually, I feel like I know everything...about...everything," Nel giggled, and gently caressed Taire's face. Her hand was surprisingly soft and warm.

    "Are you ready, Child of The Unity?"
    "How did you know?"

    "As I just said, I feel like I know everything. Also, you are the image of your ancestors, Taire. You are a Taire, are you not?" Clint was ecstatic - he zipped around the lab chirping. Nel was sassy and he loved it.

    "How?" Taire repeated.
    "Let me show you."

    "You're really not what I expec..." Before he could finish his sentence, Taire was drawn into Nel's deep-green eyes... his mind was absorbed into the deciphered virtual reality files of the archives. He was back in the caves of Raktar, witnessing what he somehow knew was the creation of the conscious mind. The Creator was huddled over a workstation. The cave walls all around him were scribed with formulae and equations.

"You did it I see, impressive work Taire. Then again, I would expect nothing less from a descendent of my family." The Creator straightened and turned to face Taire. It was the old man from the cave.

"Your family?" Taire was more than a little shook.

"Yes Taire, my family is your family, and you are exactly where, (or more accurately *when)*, you need to be. This is the day of the creation of the First Child of The Unity."

"How can we even be here, talking? This event took place thousands of years ago."

"The construction of the conscious mind opened up many possibilities, such as this one."

"But, you were in this same cave. We met here before. You said you were Raktar."

"That was not me Taire. We have not met until this moment. The apparition you encountered in the cave was in fact a manifestation of the planet's sentience. Raktar needs you to succeed, so it took on a relatable form." Taire had so many questions, though he could sense that they would have to wait. He was here for a specific reason.

"Now, are you ready to witness the birth of the First?"

"What? Er...yes, of course," Taire answered. The Creator collected the conscious mind from his crude workstation, and began to walk away.

"Well, are you coming?"

Taire hurried after him - they rounded a corner and stood before a dark alcove. The Creator placed the palm of his hand on the cave wall, and the alcove was illuminated by the warm glow of gems embedded in the rock.

"Tecta!" Taire gasped, involuntarily.

"Yes Taire, you know him. RPU Fourteen?"

"Of course the First was Tecta! How could I have been so stupid...how can he not know?"

"The key," said the Creator.

"You must use the key to awaken him to his true purpose."

"But...he has gone, and no one knows where."

"Taire, there is always a way to find that which is thought to be lost. Remember your words to your brother: *I believe anything is possible.* Now you must leave here and deliver the key to RPU Fourteen."

"Will I be able to return here? I have so many questions."

"I should very much like to speak further with you, if The Unity allows."

Taire was back in the lab onboard his ship. He was greeted by Nel's beaming smile, Sanvar's confused, semi-nauseous expression, and the happy chirps of Clint.

"Did you find what you needed Taire?"

"Thank you Nel, I did. We have a challenge ahead. I need to find Tecta."

"Vuuurrgh."Clint's tone changed dramatically.

"I know my friend, but we can do this. Nel, will you help us?"

"One second please. Tecta…" Nel looked a little vacant as she accessed the archives. Suddenly, her eyes snapped wide open, shining with wonder, "YES! YES! YES! I'm going to meet RPU Fourteen! Excuse my over excitement...but WOW!" Nel's response bolstered Clint - her optimism and enthusiasm was infectious.

Chapter Fifteen

God's God

"God, forgive my prying. Why is this Mech's engagement in our dealings here so important to you?"

"As my most trusted advisor, I will share with you a secret. Just as you worship me."

"Always, my God."

"I also have a deity to whom I have sworn my allegiance." Daa'Shond's expression grew curious.

"Surely there are none more godly than you, my lady?"

"My God has no limitations. I have faith that my God will honour my patience and subservience, and that she will return and free me from the shackles that bind me to this rock."

"Forgive my ignorance, my lady God, but what does this have to do with the Mech Warrior?"

"She needs it contained."

"Then why not let it kill itself?"

"She needs it alive. It is a small part of a vaster plan. We are not bringing warriors here purely for my amusement - we are building her a warrior army..."

"Gracious God, please excuse my ignorance once more. But the losers, they all die in the arena. So how are we building an army?"

"All is not as it seems Daa'Shond. Not all

of them die, and if they are impressive enough and salvageable, I have them revived. They are kept in stasis, so they do not spoil over time. She will need them at the peak of their ferocity."

"What! How did I not know of this?"

"Enough! Do not question the methods of your God."

"Apologies, most fearsome God. I need not know everything. I will remember my place. May I be so bold as to ask where this mighty being dwells, and when she will return?"

"No one truly knows. You must have belief…" she hissed, "I have revealed to you enough for now. I grow weary of your questions. Now take your leave, keep what has been spoken of here a secret, unless you wish to become the next *Shaar*."

"As you wish. Please remember I am always here to listen, my lady God."

Daa'Shond's twisted mind was working overtime. There had to be an angle here that he could exploit for his own personal gain. He needed to know what manner of being his God's own God was, and how to win their favour. *After all this time and effort* he thought, *God is merely a middle man*. "Mwah!" he laughed. *Tecta must know something of this* he said to himself, as he headed to Tecta's cell.

Chapter Sixteen

The Dawn Wars

Onboard The Seeker; Orbiting the Moon Treygar

Taire was overwhelmed by immersive imagery, completely enveloped once again in the ancient Raktarian archives. He was in the midst of Unity's earliest history, before the reign of the House of Royals. Taire was seeing a lost part of the galaxy's existence. A part that came before Tecta was renamed and redeployed as RPU Fourteen. He was witnessing the Dawn Wars.

Explosions of energy and plasma raged across the ancient city-scape. He recognised the city: it was the now ancient ruins on Unity. The lavish architecture, (which was painstakingly hand-carved and assembled by feats of ingenious engineering), drew no mercy or respect from the attacking droids. They knew nothing of art or beauty, only death and destruction. They ruthlessly destroyed everything without prejudice. The Unitians had not been prepared for this latest savage offensive. By now, they should have learned to expect the unexpected. At this point, the Dawn Wars had been raging for two hundred years. Tecta was present in this horrifying scene; he was front and centre, commanding the droids and raining storms of fire down upon Unity. But this wasn't Taire's Tecta - this was a hollow, soulless, death machine...

He had always believed that Tecta had been created during the Dawn Wars, for the purpose of defending Unity. It was now apparent that his origins were far darker. Tecta had been created by something else. He was one of many war machines - weapons of unprecedented ferocity. As Taire had recently learned, the conscious mind had been invented by his own ancestors. This is the point at which Tecta had become a Royal Protector Droid: the original child of Unity. A fact that, even after all these thousands of years, Tecta was still absolutely oblivious to.

Despite all that was being revealed to him, Taire was irked. It seemed that a crucial event was missing... a gaping dark hole in the archives. Something of monumental significance had happened, which had paved the way to peace and the rise of the House of Royals. A darkness lay in the background, in the void where this event should be. There was an eerie feeling... a presence almost. Whatever had happened, it had been very well hidden.

Before they became Protectors, it appeared that the droids were mindless drones born from darkness, but who did they serve before they were made sentient and developed a conscience? They betrayed whoever they had served, and chose to serve the planets and people of The Unity. They had been instrumental in bringing their ex-commander down and maintaining peace. Maybe the spark of darkness in Tecta, when he ordered the attack on Feer'aal, woke the dark memories of his first years before consciousness? Or maybe he just had a deep foreboding that he couldn't shake off, where he had convinced himself that he had to leave The Unity - in order to prevent the darkness within him turning all Protectors against the light of the galaxy once more? He would never oppose or bring harm to his children. Taire couldn't know the answers. He had to find Tecta; only he could deny or confirm any of this, and Taire now had the key to unlock this knowledge for him.

Taire was back in his lab on The Seeker. Nel's green eyes looked deep into his own.

"Are you alright Taire? You were immersed for an uncommonly long time."

"Yes I'm fine, thank you Nel."

"You seem troubled, what did you see?"

"Too much to relay."

"May I try?" asked Nel. She was asking permission to see if she could find any clues to Tecta's whereabouts in the archives. She didn't want to step on Taire's toes. Nel fell still and silent. After what seemed like an age, her eyes snapped open.

"Got it," she chirped, in her ever-cheery manner. "RPU Fourteen, or should I say Tecta, is on the battle rock of Antipathy, in the Third System." She looked dazed and preoccupied.

"You are a god-send Nel. How did you learn about Tecta's whereabouts?"

"I don't actually know. I just probed a bit and it came to me. I do feel a little odd and drained. If you'll excuse me, I think I'll shut my systems down for a while."

"Okay, thank you Nel," said Taire. He was worried that he may have been working her too hard after her long period of inactivity in the caves of Raktar.

"Taire, I've located Antipathy and I'm laying in a course now," said Sanvar, who was finally getting used to the bizarre sensations of space travel.

"Excellent Sanvar. Clint, we're bringing Tecta home."

Chapter Seventeen

Eve of the Planned Destruction

"Good evening Bear. I have been confronted with a curiosity. I believe you might be able to shed some light on it, especially as you seem to be coming around to the way of things here on Antipathy."

"I'll admit, there is a certain charm to this place... and this winning feeling... what did you want to ask me?"

"Have you, in your many years of existence, ever encountered a supremely powerful, god-like being. One who has a particular interest in you?"

"I have met many a being that believes they are of such standing. They are usually deluded and ultimately defeated. I have known none with a specific interest in me or my kind. Why do you ask?"

"It is not overly important, just a curiosity. However, if anything does come to mind, I trust you will bring it to my attention. I have brought your small friend back to you, to keep you company."

"Thank you, I do appreciate the company."

"As I said in the beginning, you will need a friend here, and now you have two." Daa'Shond grinned, and took his leave.

* * * * * * * * * *

"Did you learn anything, friend Runt?" Tecta was quick to ask the question, as soon as Daa'Shond was gone.

"Daa'Shond, him control in and out warriors."

"You mean the cells?"

"Yes friend, cells and arena."

"Tomorrow, if I cause a distraction, do you think you can get to those controls?"

"Runt can do dis thing. Him make Runt watch all fight with him."

"Thank you, friend Runt. Here's what I need you to do..."

* * * * * * * * * *

Taire instructed Sanvar to guide The Seeker into a cloud of nebulous gases, within scanning distance of Antipathy. Here they would be obscured from the view of the battle rock's sensors. From their vantage point, the rock looked benign and unimpressive, just a regular asteroid. Rigorous scanning, and the studying of magnified visuals, revealed that this was far from the case. The surface was littered with sensors and force-fields, some of which appeared to be holding parts of the structure together. After studying every inch of the scanned data, Clint finally identified a possible way in. There was a single blind spot on the surface - it would have to do.

Taire set The Seeker down on the dark side of Antipathy.

"Okay, Nel and I are going to get inside and survey the area. You two sit tight and monitor our body cams. If you spot anything we miss, any advantage, or something that could give us the upper hand, tell us immediately." Clint protested, making all kinds of unpleasant noises.

"I know you want to come too, but I need you here with Sanvar. You two will have to locate us and get us out when the time is right."

"Don't worry Clint, we... I will take care of him," said Nel.

"What was that?" asked Taire.

"Just a glitch, nothing to worry about."

"Are you sure?"

"Yes, it was nothing. We should go."

"Clint, Sanvar, stay alert, and wait for word from us."

Chapter Eighteen

The Nothing II

The Core Loway ambled to a silent halt. No impressive bangs or explosions, it just eased to a standstill.

"Pilots alive," whispered Pilot.

"Dis not so bad," said the croaky Pilot, "Pilot think Pilots die, big boom."
Pilot pushed the exit button and the Loway hatch hissed open. The air outside was dry, and all was quiet and dark.

"Where Pilots be?" asked the rotund Pilot.

"Pilot not know," said Pilot. A flame flickered in the distance, a faint glow in the misty darkness.

"Pilot go look see. Pilots come?" asked Pilot. He already knew his companions' answer.

"No!" they said in unison, "Pilots guard Loway," said the croaky Pilot.

"Why Pilot have do all things?"

Pilot sighed and set off towards the distant light. He heard the hissing of the hatch closing behind him and turned to see his nervy companions with their faces squished on the glass, waving back at him.

Pilot no scared, he said to himself, as he pushed on through the dry mist. He heard strange animal-like calls and whispered voices within the gloom around him, but he pressed on towards the warm orange hue. '*Pilot fine, no thing be scared*'. He broke out into a jolly whistle to distract his racing mind. After what seemed like an age - the mist broke. Pilot found himself standing on warm sand; a row of simple torches blazed, lighting the way to an ancient-looking tribal tent. It looked like a long-forgotten relic from another age, fashioned from scarlet velvet and golden ropes. Pilot was confused by the scene, and by what it even meant, but if there was one thing Pilot had learned since his first meeting with the Siblings, it was that everything happened for a reason. He was confident that this was the case now. Pilot approached the tent and stepped boldly inside. He found himself immersed in a gigantic living representation of the galaxy. He stared in awe and wonder at the miracle of the worlds of The Unity, dancing around the life-giving sun. They moved in all manner of curious orbits.

"Welcome, master of the Core Loway," spoke a warm, gentle voice which filled Pilot's ears.
"Hello, Pilot no see you."
"To see us is not important, but you must hear us."
"What dis place here?" Pilot asked.
"This is the point in space and time that the sentient planets meet and commune as one."
"Pilot think, Pilot understand."
"You must help Tecta and Taire."
"Friend Tecta gone, friend Taire gone too."
"We will show you where they can be found." The surroundings changed... a honeycomb- scarred asteroid loomed above him.
"Where dis rock is?" asked Pilot.

"It is named Antipathy, and it lies in the Korrix system. A part of the third. We must also tell you that Taire believes Tecta to be the final child of The Unity. He is already on his way to Antipathy. Pilot, you must get there quickly, as Taire has already arrived!"

"But, Pilot no way get there, dis not Loway route," he scratched his head in confusion "...And, Tecta Unity child?"

"Pilot, there is no time to explain, you are master of the Core Loway. You can command the Loway routes to lead anywhere. This place is called The Nothing because it does not exist in the conventional, physical sense. It is the gateway to take the Loway wherever you wish it to lead."

"Why Pilot not know dis?" He screwed up his face, clearly disgruntled.

"We are responsible. In our stubbornness we have kept it hidden, disguised as a dead end, a forbidden zone. But you are ready. We just hope we have not left it too late. The Raize are upon us. If we fail to stop them, our galaxy will die, starting with Unity herself. The fate of our galaxy will suffer the same fate as your own world of Home". Pilot's heart sank: no species should ever have to endure the hell that had befallen Home and his people. He swallowed hard, in an attempt to suppress the gut-wrenching feelings that churned in the pit of his tiny stomach. "Pilot, we need you to help Tecta and Taire make their escape, and lead them through the Loway routes. They must exit the Loway before you reach Feruccian space. There they will join The Unity ship Hope. Pilot, you must then return to the Core Loway, and wait."

"Pilot wait for what?"

"You will know when the moment arrives."

"Okay, Pilot confused some, but Pilot do dis." His familiar toothy grin, which had been absent since Tecta had left, was now on full display. Pilot puffed his chest out proudly - he had a real mission and real purpose.

"There is no time to waste. Go now. For peace, friend Pilot."

* * * * * * * * * *

Pilot stood at the Loway hatch - it hissed open. He couldn't recall how he had arrived back there, but he did remember what he had to do next. His fellow Pilots, despite their less than honourable behaviour earlier, were relieved to see their friend was safe.

"Where Pilot go?"

"Pilots have new mission."

"What mission dis?" asked croaky Pilot.

"Pilots need help friends Taire and Tecta."

"How Pilots do dis huh?" said the rotund Pilot.

"Planets they alive, speak, Pilot ask, and they help Pilots find," Pilot answered.

"This wow, Pilot need tell Nataalu."

"No time tell no one, Pilots must go now."

"Go where?"

"Through dis Nothing, to Antipatee."

"What dis Antipatee huh?"

"Pilots find out together."

Chapter Nineteen

Fight Three

The same two joyless Sectoids led Tecta along the now familiar route to the arena once again. He knew he could overpower them quite easily and make a break for freedom, but that would be too easy. There was much more than his freedom at stake here, he needed to see the plan through. Runt had been collected by Daa'Shond and taken to his usual spot in God's viewing suite. The door hissed open, and Tecta was greeted by the rapturous sound of his own name being chanted, by the crowds that were amassed inside. He had quickly become the people's champion, and he loathed it with every fibre of his being. He had to put his own feelings aside and play the game, if he and Runt's plan was going to succeed. He stepped over the threshold, threw his arms into the air, and fired off a few blaster bolts for effect. He discreetly looked for Pilot, who was exactly where he needed to be.

"Today my loyal subjects, I ask *you* the people, who do you wish to see face the Iron Bear? He has defeated the mighty Kaa'Lash. Who do you think would be a fitting opponent?" God herself addressed the gathered.
The crowds decision was unanimous: their voices erupted as one.
"Tanque! Tanque! Tanque!"

"Very well. You, the people, have spoken."
God turned to Daa'Shond and hissed, "Release
Tanque."

"Is that really such a good idea, my lady
God?" Daa'Shond was clearly not a fan of this
choice.

"Just do as I command," God snapped.

"Very well." Daa'Shond reluctantly pushed
a button on the cell console, and the crowd
fell deadly silent. A long moment passed, and
a quaking thud shook the entire arena, then
there came another and another.

"What manner of thing do you pit against
me now?" shouted Tecta.

"You will see soon enough," cackled God.
The sound of pneumatic workings hissed and
revealed a huge alternate entrance to the
arena. The entire wall became a massive
doorway. A colossal creature loomed in
silhouette. The giant door snapped shut behind
it and revealed the creature's appearance in
finer detail. It was utterly hideous; like a
mountain range of muscle, fat and ooze. It
roared... drool and rancid breath filled the
arena.

"Tanque will bring you death, tiny robot."
said Tanque, his baritone shook the ground in
equal measure to his thunderous footfalls.

"Tanque can try," was Tecta's deliberately
cocky response.

Tanque's fist, which was the same size as
Tecta himself, slammed into him. It was like
running into a wall, but the wall was doing
the running, not him. Tecta was dazed by the
impact. He engaged evasive manoeuvres. His
systems would now predict Tanque's sluggish,
but equally deadly attacks, and react
accordingly. He needed to concentrate on a

plan of attack. He was at a loss as to how he could inflict any kind of damage on Tanque, let alone defeat him. Tanque's swinging fists persisted in their sluggish pursuit of the nimble droid. There was no other choice. He needed to become the missile-like thing that he had been when he launched himself from Unity. It was an unorthodox use of 'hibernation mode', but it could just work. Tecta melded into 'sarcophagus mode', and split all power between his aft boosters and front shields. He rocketed towards Tanque's centre; the resulting impact was enough to lift the mobile landmass that was Tanque off his feet, and dump him back down on his backside. Tecta was thrown backwards by the sheer density of Tanque, and involuntarily, he reverted back to his regular form. He shook his head, dazed once again, preparing for the next incoming attack. Instead, he heard a deep guttural laugh... the thunderously joyous sound vibrated through his whole being.

"You fight good tiny droid, you have Tanque's respect. Tanque not fight you no more." Tanque remained on the floor of the arena, in a sitting protest, and his booming laughter continued.

"You both know the rules, if you refuse to fight, you will die," hissed God.

"Tanque not fight the tiny robot no more. Maybe Tanque fight you instead."

"Bear! Kill him!!" screeched Daa'Shond.

"You know the consequences if you don't," said God.

"I've lost my appetite for this game." Tecta smiled up at God.

"Sectoids, attack!" she screamed. A flood of Sectoids immediately swelled into the arena.

    "I hate to say I told you so, but I did
tell you not to choose Tanque."

    "Shut up Daa'Shond. Bear! Attack
him...NOW!"

    "I don't think so. I want to see how this
one plays out."
Tanque was on his feet, swinging his massive
fists and decimating scores of Sectoids. Tecta
was also cutting swathes through the onrushing
horde.

Taire and Nel had successfully infiltrated the
battle rock, and their task had been made
easier by the fact that every single occupant
of Antipathy was crammed into the arena. The
two of them looked on from the sweaty, stench-
ridden press of the crowd. They had watched
and waited anxiously for the opportune moment
to intervene. That moment was about to arrive.
Tanque forced his massive bulk upward and
swung a wrecking ball of a fist, which smashed
through the rock that was fused with God's
gigantic body – and it slammed devastatingly
into her exposed torso. The whole arena shook
violently; the combination of Tanque's
landing, and the jolt of God's movement,
caused the entire environment to quake. The
powerful tremors disguised the arrival of the
Loway pod, burrowing up through the arena.

    "Friends, Pilot here save you." Pilot
struggled to make himself heard above the
carnage. That didn't matter, as Tecta had
spotted the Loway pod. Taire was already
headed toward Pilot. Nel's component parts
buzzed and ripped through the arena, cutting
down the last of the Sectoids. Their broken
bodies littered the floor left, right and
centre.

Up in the viewing suite, God appeared to be
delirious from the vicious assault of Tanque.
    "But, you promised to return and free me."
    "To whom are you speaking?" asked
Daa'Shond.
    "Can you not hear her? She speaks..." came
God's reply.
    "I hear nothing. Not only have you lost
your mind, you've lost control of everything."
God wasn't hearing Daa'Shond, the only words
she heard were...
    "...*I have freed you.*" The Dark Mother's voice
invaded God's mind.
    "Nooo! Not like this! Show yourself," God
screamed.

* * * * * * * * * *

Runt had made the most of the distractions. In
a frenzied panic, he had hit every button on
Daa'Shond's controls. A piercing alarm
sounded, and the whole side of the arena
hissed open, exposing the blindingly-lit
opening Tanque had used to enter the arena.
Scores of silhouettes of all shapes and sizes
appeared.
    "I take it this wasn't part of your
imaginary deity's plan?" scoffed Daa'Shond.
    "Dark Mother, why have you forsaken me?"
God's eyes bulged in terror. They reflected
the sight of the onrushing silhouettes of the
warriors, that had burst from the back-lit
opening in the arena. They joined Tanque in
attacking God. Some scaled her massive torso,
biting and slashing at her exposed, scaly skin

with ferocious claws and teeth. Tanque's fists swung like twin wrecking balls - pounding at her. The impacts penetrated deeply, cracking the ancient, dense skeleton which lay deep beneath her vast covering of leathery flesh and fat.

"Daa'Shond, help me!" God shrieked.

"You have been played for a fool. I will not perish here for your mistakes. I bid you goodbye," Daa'Shond sneered. His only thought now was to save his own skin. He turned to run, pausing only briefly to collect Runt. But Runt was gone; he had fled at the blast of the alarm, and was weaving his way through the chaos and broken bodies of the defeated Sectoids below, to get to Tecta.

"Friend Tecta, dis place broken," warned Runt. "We go now." Runt was right - the crowds had already evacuated. The arena had fallen silent. The only sound was the thud, crack and squelch of Tanque's relentless blows making contact with God's mutilated body. Even the freed warriors had fled after briefly attacking God.

A dense, black, blaster bolt sizzled through the air and broke the eerie silence. It hurtled towards Tecta. "NO!" screamed Taire, as he launched Ki'resh. The ring intercepted the blaster bolt, redirecting its course away from Tecta. He chased after the ring to join his friend.

"Taire! I don't want to do this. She is forcing me." Taire looked in the direction of the voice - it was Nel - she had fired the bolt. She was clearly distressed. She became suddenly still, and her expression turned dark and malevolent.

"Now that I have your attention drone. Do

you not recognise your own Mother?" Nel's voice was not her own - she was being controlled by something else entirely, something that oozed darkness and threat. "I am set free to take revenge on my ungrateful, treacherous children, and destroy all that you hold dear. This body is powerful enough to do my will. You see, my son, I only need to concern myself with destroying you. The rest is already taken care of. Your beloved Unity is in for a rather unpleasant surprise." Her tone carried a bitter tang, like the burn of a superior mustard hitting your tongue.

"This is clearly a case of mistaken identity. I have never seen or heard of you before now. But, I will stop you." Tecta engaged 'attack mode', and fired a volley of bolts at Nel's body. One enemy became six. As Nel's component parts were deployed, each piece spun through the musty air, becoming an intelligent, spherical weapon in its own right.

Taire used Ve'dow to create a force-field around Tecta, Runt and himself. He sent Ki'resh on an attack run, which ricocheted between Nel's spheres. Their armoured shells were too dense for the rings to slice through at any useful pace. He and his friends needed another plan.

"This is a psychological attack," Taire blurted out the revelation, as soon as it had entered his head. "Just like The Hushed used. Something else is controlling her body. We need to sever The Link." Get her inside the Loway Pod: the Tek will nullify the mind invasion."

"We cannot force her inside. We need to lure her..." was Tecta's response.

"Tecta, she is too intelligent to fall for that. We only need to get one of the spheres inside; if we can do that, the others will fall. We need to divide their attention."

Taire had hatched a plan. He gave Runt his instructions. He then sent Ki'resh on another attack run, this time focusing the O blade's full force on a single sphere. It spun furiously, like a grinder cutting at the armoured surface. Tecta concentrated his fire on that same sphere. The other spheres turned their attention to the single sphere that was under attack, redirecting their fire on Ki'resh.

Runt made his move. He ran across the arena to Tanque, who was still pummelling at God's now utterly dead body. Nel's spheres ignored Runt completely, as far as the Dark Mother was concerned, the insignificant being was of no consequence in this fight. Once Runt had reached Tanque, he clambered up the terrain of his legs, on to his back, and then up on to his shoulder to deliver his message.

Tecta aimed his blasters at the sphere closest to Tanque. Its turret switched aim from Ki'resh, and instead focused on Tecta.
    "Now Runt!" shouted Taire. Tanque swung his boulder of a fist at the oblivious sphere... the impact launched it towards the Loway Pod. Tecta ran towards the pod, like an athlete in the biggest race of his life. He launched himself across the arena, and grabbed the dazed sphere as it sped through the air. With a blast of his boosters, he powered through the hatch and into the Loway Pod. The effects of the Loway's Tek shield were

instantaneous. Nel's spheres crashed to the floor and transformed into their original component parts, before eerily sliding to the Loway Pod, where they reassembled to complete Nel's lifeless form.

Tanque gently lowered Runt to the ground in the palm of his giant hand.

"Tanque do good?" his voice boomed.

"Thank you Tanque, you did great. Now you need to get out of here. This place is falling apart." said Taire.

"Tanque sleep now. Tanque tired."

"But you will die if you stay here." there was genuine concern in Taire's voice.

"Tanque not die, just sleep and float space till find new home." Runt and Taire bid a brief farewell to Tanque, and boarded the Loway Pod. No sooner had the hatch shut, the pod was away. They caught a brief glimpse of Tanque cannonballing his way out of Antipathy and into space.

"Safe travel, friend Tanque," said Runt.

"Clint, Sanvar, you need to get away from here now," Taire shouted into the comms.

"On it," came Sanvar's reply.

"Rendezvous with us at the nebula."

"But, how did you get out?"

"Long story, you need to trust me. Look for a portal, a spacial distortion. Fly directly into it. We'll see you on the inside."

Antipathy was shattering. The movement of God had torn the battle rock apart, and the emitters that bound the surface of the rock together had failed. The gargantuan space rock Antipathy had disintegrated, creating a

massive debris field. The Seeker powered
through the scattered obstacles, weaving this
way and that, to dodge the multitude of rocks
and flash-frozen corpses that spun through the
space all around them. Sanvar had given
control of the vessel to Clint, as he was far
too inexperienced to pilot the ship through a
debris field of this magnitude or density.
Instead, he took control of the weapons
systems and began blasting a path through the
dense rocks. The Seeker took a few scrapes and
dents, but they were almost clear. Clint
chirruped - he could see the spatial anomaly
ahead. It looked like a heat haze, warping the
star-fields beyond it. Once they emerged from
the debris field, Clint engaged maximum
thrusters and headed straight for the anomaly.
The Seeker was swiftly swallowed up. Sanvar
was completely disorientated, due to the ship
being surrounded by rushing light and colour.

    "Clint, where are we?" asked Sanvar.

    "Bleept blunkt," was Clint's reply.

    "Welcome Core Loway, friends. Me Pilot,"
Pilot's voice came through the comms. "We
maglock you ship now, you come Loway."

    "Okay…" replied Sanvar, tentatively.

    "Sanvar, it's me Taire. Don't worry, Pilot
is a trusted friend." Clint trilled with
excitement at hearing Taire's voice.

    "It's good to hear you too Clint. I'm so
relieved you both made it out in one piece."
The maglock engaged with a metallic clunk, and
The Seeker's door opened. Taire and Pilot were
inside the Hangar Bay to greet them.

    "Where is Nel?" was Sanvar's first
question.

Chapter Twenty

Defence of Unity I

Zee, Zero-Nine and Mardran laughed and joked
as they patrolled the outer borders of new
Unity Space. They performed the usual
protocols under the ever-serious gaze of
Seventeen. His manner had grown even more
severe since Tecta had disappeared. The crew
were fully aware that their overly-meticulous
scanning was performed in the hope of locating
Tecta.

"Although we all know that we are out here
on a hopeless mission, at least *happy* over
there has kept the team together," Zero-Nine
nodded in Seventeen's direction.

"Will your feud ever stop?" laughed Zee.

"I hope not. That would make this quite
the boring existence...unless you have
reconsidered my proposal Zee," laughed Zero-
Nine.

"You really don't know when you're
defeated, do you Zero?" Mardran laughed. She
approached Zee and kissed her full on the
mouth.

"I believe this is a breach of protocol,
not to mention highly unprofessional," Zero
smiled. He knew Zee would never regard him
with the same passion that she had for
Mardran. Still - they were firm friends who
had developed a bond way beyond the physical,
even if he did still harbour fantasies and

desires.

"Actually, would it be totally out of the question if us three have a polyamo..."

"Yes," Zee snapped.

"Totally out of the question!" added Mardran.

"You can't blame a droid for trying," mumbled Zero.

Seventeen smirked quietly to himself as he listened to the exchanges of his crew. He would never let on, but he enjoyed their playful banter and their company. He was well aware that they thought him to be grumpy and harsh, miserable even. What they didn't know was that he wholeheartedly believed in their mission, and he had a constant, gut- wrenching feeling that it was imperative that they find Tecta. Seventeen didn't know why or how, but he was convinced that something very ominous was lurking over the horizon and they all needed to be ready. More importantly, they needed Tecta. His old friend was the key to preventing what would happen next.

"What is that?" Mardran stood agog - displayed on the view screen were two massive spatial pulses that emanated from Raktar and Unity; the two pulses came together to link as one. The union was brief, but dazzling and vibrant.

"Unity, come in. this is Seventeen. What is happening there?"

"Hope, this is Thirty-Two. We have experienced an abnormal planetary energy surge, but all is now back within expected parameters." An alarm blared deafeningly on the bridge.

"Seventeen, multiple readings."

said Zero.

"What position?"

"Everywhere! They appear to be very rude. They seem to have no interest in us at all." Zero replied.

"Well, what are they interested in?" snapped Seventeen.

"They appear to be on a heading for Unity." Zero's voice carried concern.

"What manner of vessels are they? Match their pace and course, continue scanning them. We need to know what we are dealing with."

"All over it," chirped Zero.

"Mardran, alert Unity that they have unknowns incoming... a lot of them."

"Seventeen, you need to see this. I think my eyes deceive me." Zero was uncommonly shaken. Seventeen approached the console and stopped in his tracks.

"Mardran!" he yelled, "Issue a maximum alert to Unity. Tell them The Raize are approaching. All available Protector Droids are to brief all personel and share all intel that they have on The Raize. There is not a second to spare. Scramble all available fighters. Brief pilots and crews while they equip and launch - stopping The Raize in space is our only chance. They must not be allowed to make landfall."

"On it now!" Mardran spoke, with urgency. Zee turned to Zero-Nine.

"Who are The Raize?"

"We had hoped nobody would ever need to know. They were thought to be extinct," Zero replied. "They are vile, energy-leeching creatures; they have bled countless worlds dry. Over five hundred years ago we journeyed to the Third System to answer a distress call.

By the time we arrived - millions had perished... all that remained of the breached planets were withered husks and devastated shells, where vibrant worlds had once thrived. We allied ourselves with the last two surviving worlds. Together we made a stand: and pushed them back.

"We completely eradicated them...or so we had thought. Until this moment, we had believed them to be extinct. The Raize had never made it to our system, or Unity Space," Seventeen explained. His pained expression said so much more than his words. This situation was beyond bad.

"There is no time to linger on what has passed, we need to stop them now." ordered Seventeen.

"How do we do that exactly?" Zee asked.

"Whilst they are in space, they are vulnerable." said Seventeen.

"They are single-minded in their mission; like sperm racing to an egg. However, their aim is not to reproduce, it is to destroy - no distractions." said Zero

"Zero's overly-graphic description is accurate. This is also their flaw; they will not retaliate, as the harvest is their sole reason for being. We need to start taking them out now. All hands to weapons stations. Our fleet back home is going to need all the help that they can get. We need to eliminate as many of their number as we can." said Seventeen.

"They must have been triggered by the burst of energy from Unity. They feed on planetary energy." Zero voiced his theory.

"Indeed, like moths to a flame. But these things are not moths, nothing so benign." The severity in Seventeen's tone unsettled Zee and Mardran.

"But, how are they back?" asked Zero.

"It doesn't matter. Less talking, more shooting!" snapped Seventeen.

"Locked and loaded." Zero gripped the controls of the rapid pulse cannon and screamed, "DIE!" His shots ripped through The Raize, reducing them to ashen embers that dispersed into space - to drift for eternity...

"Great shooting Zero, but maybe take the screaming down a touch."

"It is my battle cry Seventeen, try it, you might like it."

"I'll stick to my own methods thank you."

"DIE!" Zero screamed again. Seventeen shook his head, muted his aural processors, and went about exterminating The Raize. Mardran was not only keeping pace with the alien swarm; she was skilfully using The Hope itself as a weapon, slicing into shoals of them. Zee unleashed heavy charges into their midst, taking out dozens at a time. Seventeen and Zero's precise laser blasts tore through wave after wave of the relentless aliens, like swordfish cutting through a sea of silver waves. The Raize, predictably, did not respond. They just continued to rush onward to their target. Disregarding their attackers, they relied on sheer numbers and perseverance to meet their objective.

The swarm entered Slaavene space, and rapidly approached the red and grey planet. A huge attack force peeled away from the surface of the planet. A tsunami of fighters looped under the swarm to join The Hope. The Slaavene opened fire on The Raize - a blazing wall of fury ripped into the swarm.

"Yeah! Woooo Hooooooo!" whooped Zero.

"Captain Raxnelle, boy are we ever glad to see you and your fleet," said Zero, who recognised his ship, The Marauder, from the battle of Mora.

"Together, for peace," was the emotionless response that came back through the comms. The Slaavene never had been a very communicative species, but they were formidable warriors, and very welcome allies.

The smaller, more nimble Slaavene attack ships broke free of the fleet, and headed deep into the heart of The Raize swarm. The attack ships detonated pulse disruptors and ended scores of The Raize. With every pulse, vast numbers of The Raize were disintegrated, and the embers of their remains drifted away to join the myriad of entities that dwelled in the Afterverse.

"We might actually be able to do this."

"To what part of 'this' do you refer, Zero-Nine?" said Seventeen.

"Have you malfunctioned on some level? What other part of 'this' is there? Stopping The Raize...obviously."

"Rudeness is not a virtue, Zero."

"Neither is idiocy, Seventeen."

"Will you two just give it a rest, or get a room," snapped Zee.

"Jealous?" sniped Zero.

"In your dreams," laughed Mardran.

"Always," Zero replied, with a satisfied grin that lit up his whole face.

"Just keep firing," commanded Seventeen - he had grown weary of the infantile conversation.

Blaammmm. The Hope took a hit to its aft deflectors. The freshly-destroyed remnants of a Slaavene ship had slammed into them. A new element had joined the fray, and they were intent on attacking The Unity forces. God's Attack Drones had been deployed to give The Raize a fighting chance to complete their mission.

"Raxnelle, we have incoming at six o'clock."
"We have detected the enemy Seventeen, and we are preparing to engage. Are you hit?"
"Shields are holding." Another blast was incoming... Mardran barrel-rolled The Hope, and then she threw her into a diving loop, pulling out of the loop directly underneath the enemy.
"Have you got weapons lock?" she called to her crew mates. The answer to her question came in the form of an explosion of enemy ships. She tinted the view screen to dull the glare of the blinding fireball as they passed through it. The Slaavene cruisers,(including The Marauder), had mirrored The Hope's manoeuvre and attacked the drones from above. The drones scattered erratically, like a pack of spooked Rangmouse that had just spotted a predator. But they would not go down without a fight. The tenacious crafts performed intricate manoeuvres - they twisted and turned, spitting vicious little spikes of plasma at the fleet. The size of the weapon's discharge was deceptive; the spikes succeeded in penetrating shields to relieve some of the ships of their surface weapons and sections of armour. This dog fight was an annoying and very unwelcome distraction, but the Drones needed to be taken care of. They were causing

a fair amount of chaos and were inflicting
some serious damage on the Slaavene cruisers.
Two had been disabled, and one was even
totally destroyed, but The Hope and the fleet
had gained the upper hand. The Drones now only
had half the number of units they had started
this fight with, but Seventeen knew this was
taking far too long.

"Zero, scan for any pockets of gaseous
matter on the moon's surface - the more vast
and dense the better."
"What are you thinking Seventeen?" asked
Zee.
"You will see very shortly," he replied.
"Marauder, is there anyway that you can
shepherd them to the following coordinates?"
Seventeen reeled off the numbers.
"Yes, but what purpose does it serve
directing them to the moon of Veenar?"
"Trust me, I have a plan. Drive them as
close to the moon's surface as you can, but do
not enter the atmosphere. Be ready to retreat
as soon as I give the command."
"Understood."
The Slaavene fleet were forming the Drones
into a cluster, forcing them towards the given
coordinates.
"Go on, take the bait. You know it makes
sense," said Seventeen, who was willing the
Drones to enter the moon's atmosphere.
"Seventeen, I believe I have found a
suitable candidate that fits your request."
said Zero-Nine.
"Excellent Zero." Seventeen replied.
"That's possibly the nicest thing you've…"
"Please, not now Zero. Send the
coordinates to Zee's station." said Seventeen.
The Drones behaved exactly as any self-

preserving, pre-programmed drone should. They plunged into the moon's atmosphere, with the knowledge that they were much more manoeuvrable in the atmosphere than the Slaavene cruisers. It was the logical tactic.

"Raxnelle, retreat now!" bellowed Seventeen. "Zee, fire!"

"Torpedoes away." The warheads tore through Veenar's atmosphere and penetrated the moon's rocky crust. The torpedoes detonated, igniting the sizeable pocket of subterranean gases Zero had identified. The detonation caused a catastrophic chain reaction, which in turn ignited the moon's dense gaseous atmosphere. The raging inferno that shrouded the moon incinerated every last Drone.
The bridge of The Hope was filled with a stunned silence.

"Wow, Seventeen that was…" said Zee.

"Ingenious," Raxnelle's monotone came through the comms to finish Zee's sentence.

"There is no time for celebration. We must get back to The Raize now." Snapped Seventeen.

Chapter Twenty-One

Memories

Onboard The Core Loway, Pilot was overjoyed at seeing someone who he had missed for a very long time.

He ran to Tecta and wrapped his arms around his thigh. He was like a child, reunited with a parent who had returned from a faraway conflict.

"Pilot miss you, friend Tecta."

"It's good to see you too, friend Pilot. This is friend Runt." Runt stepped out cautiously from behind Tecta.

"Him name not Pilot, like all other Pilots?" Pilot extended his flat palms in the traditional Pilot greeting, but Runt hid behind Tecta again. "Dis one different now, friend Tecta. Pilot see him not want to be Pilot. Him too long alone."

"Give him time friend."

Taire knelt on the floor, cradling Nel's lifeless body.

"Thank you all for coming for me," said Tecta. Taire looked up at him.

"Tecta, we are family. We still need you very much. We could never have made it this far. Your role in this is far from over," said Taire.

"What is that?" Tecta was distracted - he referred to the key that Taire wore on a leather thong around his neck.

"It's a key."

"I can see that," Tecta said sternly. Although he was happy to be back amongst family, he was in no mood for humour.

"Raktar gave it to me, with the intention that we use it to unlock your lost memories."

"Lost memories? I do not understand, and as for Raktar, that planet fell silent many, many years ago."

"Yes it did, but now it's waking up. The planet told me that you have hidden knowledge within your conscious mind, from a time before the Dawn Wars."

"That is impossible! I was created during the Dawn Wars to protect Unity."

"It seems that you were not. You were something else before you were made sentient."

"I am intrigued by this revelation, although I do remain highly sceptical."

"Will you permit me to install the key?"

"Of course, but be prepared for disappointment."

Taire asked Sanvar to stay with Nel incase she woke. He and Tecta retreated to the living quarters. Tecta took a seat at the circular metal table. He dropped his head forward to expose his interface. Taire pulled the key from around his neck and slid it into one of Tecta's many ports. To Taire's surprise; the key became liquid on contact with the interface, and was absorbed into Tecta's systems. Tecta closed the interface and raised his head.

"Do you feel anything different?" asked Taire.

"No!" shouted Tecta, "This cannot be! We

banished her. Her consciousness may have been set free, but she is not actually free. She is still marooned on Po'Tu, where we sent her."

"Tecta, the voice that spoke through Nel, that was the same voice that I heard in the Archive Chamber on Raktar. Was that the Dark Mother? Is it true that the Dark Mother is your Mother?" Tecta wore a haunted expression.

"Yes, she is my Mother, but only in the most base sense of the word. She created me; as she created all of us who would become the Royal Protector Droids. That is the limit of her maternal nature. Excuse my broken explanation, but my head is full of disturbing, unfamiliar memories of her."

"Tecta, I appreciate that you must be going through a whole world of confusion right now, but this is a disaster. Sanvar was supposed to learn about the New Unity and set an example to the people of Raktar; if they know that the Dark Mother is real, their belief will become more entrenched than ever."

"We have more immediate concerns Taire. Why did you not kill her with the rings?" Tecta was referring to Nel.

"There was no need. I just needed to keep her at bay while we executed the plan."

"I remember so much that was missing before. Nel must have been modified with a susceptibility chip, a trick the Dark Mother has used many times over. It enables Nel to house the consciousness of the Dark Mother. The archives have shown you exactly what the Dark Mother wanted you to see. All this was a carefully orchestrated plan to end me, and The Unity. She corrupted Nel's system with her consciousness, and used Nel's charm to seduce you Taire. Thanks to your quick thinking, we have delayed her return...for now. At some point, Po'Tu will come in to phase, and she will be at the height of her power... We must be prepared for all out war. Nel is corrupted: an unacceptable risk. She must be destroyed."

"Please Tecta no, don't do this, you cannot kill her."

"She is an abomination Taire, and as I have already said, corrupted. She must be nullified."

"But, it's not her fault and...I...I love her."

"Then you love a lie. Have you not heard anything that I have just said? You have been seduced by the vile force that has taken control of her. So this is the truth of why you did not kill her."

"No Tecta - I've been inside her mind. There is a duality. I know what is false and what is her true self. Love is love regardless, and it is no secret that I've always been more comfortable with droids than biologicals," said Taire.

"I do not question your love Taire; however, I know what's seized control of Nel, and what she plans to do if she succeeds. I will not let that happen...at any cost."

"What if I can separate them, and free Nel from her grip?"

"So how would you suggest that you do that?"

"We need to make the Tek a permanent part of Nel's systems. It will block the Dark Mother permanently."

"You can try, but if it doesn't work... I will put her down for the good of us all."

"It will not come to that," said Taire confidently.

"Very well, but she must not be allowed to leave the Loway until we are sure that the Tek is in control of her systems."

They re-joined the group in the control room.
     "Pilot, set a course to Unity, maximum
speed." Tecta commanded.
     "Pilot can no do dis, The Nothing say you
need go Feer'aal moon."
     "The Nothing?" questioned Taire.
     "Yes, friends must help Seventeen, fight
Raize." said Pilot.
     "So, what God and Runt have said is true.
The Raize are attacking. We must stop them, or
none of this will matter, as there will be no
home to return to. Pilot, take us to the first
moon of Feer'aal: there we will join our
comrades in arms." Tecta's words carried an
unsettling urgency as Mimm's face flashed into
his mind once again.

Chapter Twenty-Two

Duty

"Lu!" shouted Gliis, as he burst through his sister's chamber door. "Taire, is in danger!"

"I know Gliis, I have felt it too. I have also felt that this is Taire's mission, and his alone. He will have everything he needs. We must not intervene. What we must do is to protect the New Unity. Our brother will fulfil his own destiny. We must mind our own duties here. Gliis, we are under attack."

"From who?"

"Come, we must meet Thirty-Two in the Unity Hall. He will brief us fully on what we face."

"You can tell us all on the way Gliis, I'm intrigued to know what you have learned," Tam spoke soothingly. Gliis and Kee'Pah blurted out everything that they had learned in The Silence, as they walked along the halls.

"Kee'Pah and I have been studying The Silence; and it is no longer silent, it sings, communes with us even! We have communicated with Unity herself - she linked with Raktar and showed us images of Taire fighting in a cave. It was like the two caves were an extension of each other, but he could not see us."

"That must have been the cause of the planetary energy surge," said Tam.

"The planets have spoken to us - they are awake and reconnecting. They said that we, the Children of The Unity, must prepare." Gliis hadn't stopped talking the whole time they were walking. The only pause came just before they entered Unity Hall; the whole groups attention had been caught by the spectacle taking shape outside the large, paned windows. They drew a deep collective breath, and tore themselves away from the impressive, ever-growing fleet outside.

"Come, we need to put these pieces together and figure out exactly what is going on," said Lu.

Chapter Twenty-Three

Defence of Unity II

The sky over Unity was teeming with all manner of ships. Hornets, Defenders and Assault Rammers hurtled up toward Unity Space, soon to be joined by the next wave that were already set to launch. The Planets of the New Unity had built a formidable fleet in the years since the battle of Mora. Using shared technologies, they had created new ships and improved the capabilities of their existing craft. Not least of all - Pilot's Hornets, which had been equipped with much needed self-charging cells.

Thirty-Two passed by the long windows of the halls - he allowed himself a moment to admire the vast fleet that populated the Unity skies. He had been given command of the Protector Droids whilst Seventeen was off-world. Thirty-Two was a bland, straight -talking individual. He liked to get to the point of things quickly. This had led to him regularly coming across as blunt. Over the years, the Children of The Unity had grown used to his foibles, and they were fond of him. He entered the Unity Hall. Lu, Gliis, Tam and Kee'Pah were already gathered inside. Thirty-Two had barely made it through the door when Gliis started asking questions.

"Where is Pilot? There were only a handful

of Hornets in the fleet."

"It is unfortunate that you ask Gliis, and I regret to inform you that we have lost all contact with the Core Loway. Pilot answered our first communications, and advised they were returning to Unity to join the fleet. We have heard nothing since... despite numerous hails."

"Don't worry Gliis, Pilots can look after themselves - Fifty-Six made sure of that. They will be just fine," said Lu, trying to reassure her brother as best as she could.

"I hope you are right Lu," Gliis sighed.

"Now, may we continue?" said Thirty-Two impatiently, ~~he~~ who didn't wait for a reply. "Very good. The fleet has been briefed, and as you can see, the ships are away. The enemy, The Raize, are a uniquely disturbing species – intelligent, biological, liquid-metal entities. They must not be allowed to make landfall."

"And what happens if they do make it to Unity?" asked Kee'Pah, unsure whether she wanted to know the answer.

"They are planet killers; they will lock onto our planet's surface and absorb every last resource of Unity, like a plague of locusts. Everything will die." Thirty-Two's bluntness was in full force.

"So, what do we do if the fleet fails to stop them?" asked Tam.

"The Unity Spire," Lu replied.

"But Taire is not here," Gliis protested.

"No, he is not, but Kee'Pah and Tam are here. It is time that we test Etala's theory of the Children of The Unity."

Chapter Twenty-Four

United

Taire, Tecta and Runt boarded The Seeker, with Clint and Sanvar. The Seeker exited the Loway routes and roared through the moon's thin atmosphere, where they were met with the disorienting sight of thousands upon thousands of Raize... and the spectacle of The Hope and Slaavene fleet ripping through the bizarre creatures.

"What dis many things?" asked Runt.

"Hold course Runt! Dead ahead! The fleet needs all the firepower it can get," commanded Tecta.

"There are so many of them!" replied Taire. "They are... beautiful."

"Beautiful planet-killing demons," snapped Tecta, as he squeezed the triggers on the weapons controls, unleashing volley after volley of fiery energy bolts. Taire could feel the rage coming from Tecta; a sensation he had never witnessed before. The Raize must be truly savage to have evoked such anger in his friend and mentor. Their looks were deceptive; they appeared as a sea of silver angels, gently drifting in the solar winds... an appearance which clearly belied their true nature. They brought to mind the tales of The Sirens, from the stories Tecta used to tell the siblings as children.

"Glad you could join us," came the familiar tone of Seventeen's voice, which crackled through the comms panel.

"Yeah, get here when you can!" added Zero's voice.

"It's good to hear your voices," Taire replied.

"What is the current status of The Raize?" asked Tecta.

"They are not retaliating, which is no surprise, as you well know Tecta. Together, with the Slaavene fleet, we have cleared out an entire battalion of Attack Drones. They were of unknown origin, but were clearly here to help The Raize. They ambushed us, appeared from out of nowhere, and attacked us from the rear. The Slaavene fleet is in amongst the swarm, attacking The Raize from within. I have transmitted to you their shield modulations to prevent any friendly fire," Seventeen reported.

"I never understood that term - what's friendly about blowing up your own allies?" said Zero.

"Shut up Zero, and stop interrupting," snapped Seventeen.

"It's nice to see some things haven't changed," laughed Taire.

"Taire, get to the ventral cannon. You can talk and shoot at the same time. Runt, take us closer to the swarm," Tecta snapped. He was anxious to take out as many of The Raize as they could, before they reached The Unity fleet.

"Sorry Tecta," said Taire, a little embarrassed. He hurried to the weapons station and opened fire on the swarm.

"I apologise for my curt tone Taire. You didn't seem to be grasping the gravity of the threat these creatures carry. If we do not stop them - there will be nothing left of Unity - or your siblings."

"I understand," said Taire. In truth, he was a little hurt, and felt like the inexperienced, self-doubting boy he had been in his youth on Veela VI. But Tecta was right...as usual. He needed to focus.

"It's good to have you back Tecta," he said.

"DIE!" Zero-Nine shouted.

"Zero, will you stop that?" came the stern response from Seventeen.

"But, it helps me focus... DIE!" Comms had been left open, and Taire could still hear everything that was being said onboard The Hope. The exchange between his two friends had brought back the smile which, only moments before, had been one of embarrassment.

Chapter Twenty-Five

Survivors?

This was the moment Tecta had been quietly dreading since they re-entered New Unity Space. The planet Feer'aal came into view, and brought with it all the associated feelings of guilt and regret. They bubbled unstoppably to the surface.

"You do know you have nothing to feel guilty about," said Taire, sensing the negative change in Tecta's demeanour.

"I cannot help what I feel, much like you with your feelings towards Nel."

"In time, you will learn to be at one with it," said Taire.

"When did you become so philosophical, my child?"

"I had a good teacher; it's just a shame he doesn't always follow his own teachings." Taire smiled, and Tecta wryly returned the gesture.

Ahead of them, a luminous red energy beam tore a hole through the spearhead of the swarm. It appeared to come from out of nowhere. Zero-Nine tracked the beam to its point of origin. The sound of his shocked voice came through the comms, it broke the silence between Taire and Tecta.

"Feer'aal? Tecta, it came from Feer'aal!" exclaimed Zero.

"How is that even possible?" asked Tecta.

"There must have been survivors of Injis's attack after all," said Taire, with optimism.

"That is one theory, or it may be an automated defence system," said Tecta, trying to hide his emotion. He needed to stay focused on the task in hand. Now was not the time to process the questions that this latest event posed. If they didn't stop The Raize, it would be a moot point anyway.

The Slaavene fleet withdrew from the heart of the swarm; they didn't want to get caught up in any further energy blasts that might occur. The fleet ships formed up alongside The Seeker and The Hope. They continued the assault on the seemingly infinite number of The Raize. Another ferocious blast rocketed from Feer'aal and carved another gaping hole in the swarm.

"We need to fall back and go dark, or we will never make it past that beam," said Seventeen, addressing the Slaavene and Unity ships.

"But that will waste precious time - we need to continue our offensive," Tecta spoke angrily.

"No offence meant Tecta, but you were the one who disappeared and left the rest of us to pick up the pieces. I respectfully ask you to follow my orders, old friend."

"He has a point," added Taire, followed by, "Sorry."

"I know that you are both right Taire. I just can't help but feel that if I hadn't of left, then none of this would be happening."

"That's the most conceited thing I have ever heard you say," snapped Taire.

"I apologise. Recent events have taken a greater toll on me than I had realised."

"Stop apologising and follow Seventeen's orders." Taire felt the adrenaline rise and race through his veins. He never thought he would, or could, speak to Tecta this way. His time away had changed him more than he would care to admit.

The ships drifted on the momentum created by the thrusters, which were then swiftly cut. The fleet passed silently over Feer'aal - in a wide, staggered formation. The pace was painfully slow, each ship leaving a sizeable gap between themselves and the previous vessel. They could only watch on as the void between themselves and The Raize widened, eventually disappearing from their view completely.

Chapter Twenty-Six

The Spire of Hope

The Children of The Unity made their way to
the Unity Spire. They always travelled to the
ancient site on foot. It was like a pilgrimage
- a mark of respect. Today the pace was a
little quicker than usual. There was a sense
of understandable urgency about the group. As
they walked, they couldn't help but glance
skywards. Thirty-Two's ship was the last
vessel to depart from Unity; they watched as
it rocketed into the sky to join the final
wave of fleet ships. They were now nothing
more than tiny black specks and vapour trails
as they exited Unity's atmosphere. Their
surroundings were so peaceful and serene... it
was hard to imagine the panic that was going
on faraway in space above them. The truth of
what was actually going on up there played
heavily on the group's minds. In less than a
day, the natural beauty that surrounded them
could be reduced to nothing more than dust and
ash. The silence between the four of them
spoke volumes.

The Unity Spire lay just ahead. Although Tam
and Kee'Pah had visited the Spire many times
over the last few years, they had never come
here before with the intent of channelling its

power. As they reached their destination, there was a distinct difference in the air; an almost electric buzz. The Unity Spire hummed and pulsed with energy... There was no way of knowing whether this was a lingering after-affect of the earlier energy surge, or a sign that the Spire itself knew that the four of them had journeyed there with purpose.

Chapter Twenty-Seven

Showdown at Shinara Prime

The New Unity fleet lay in wait on the far side of Shinara Prime. The Raize were incoming; they appeared as a vast blanket of gently rippling silk on a breeze, creeping closer with every beat of their delicate wings.

"Thirty-Two to Unity fleet; this is a defining moment. We are all that stands between The Raize and the destruction of Unity. I ask you to fight with everything you have, or there will be no tomorrow for any of us. For peace...Engage!"

The wall of fire that blasted forth from the amassed fleet was comparable to the shockwave of a sun-gone-supernova. The force of the collective assault blazed through scores of The Raize, but still they came, like an endless flood.

"All ships, fire at will!" commanded Thirty-Two. Wave after wave of violence powered into the swarm.

Although it had slowed the efforts of Seventeen's fleet, the crews of all ships concerned had been replenished, by the respite provided in the need to go dark over Feer'aal. They had been relentlessly firing upon The

Raize for three days straight. They took shifts in sleeping and manning the weapons, finding no time for anything other than eating, drinking or using the toilet. The droids of course had no need for any of these distractions. They had been firing without pause for more than seventy two hours. The Raize's numbers had been greatly reduced, but there still remained more than enough of them to decimate Unity, should they succeed and make landfall.

"Seventeen to allied fleet, the Unity fleet has engaged The Raize at Shinara Prime... this is the final push. Now that we have re-engaged with the enemy, muster everything you have left within you and continue the assault. All of our futures depend on it. For peace!"

"For peace," came a chorus of voices through the comms.

"Yessss! Let's make a Raize sandwich!" yelled Zero, followed by his now familiar battle cry, "DIE!!!"

The Unity fleet blockade stood resolute in the face of the swarm, releasing wave after wave of deadly fire, whilst their smaller, more nimble ships entangled themselves among the swarm with the Slaavene vessels: victory was at hand.

"Stop celebrating. We have been out-manoeuvred," yelled Zero-Nine. I am detecting numerous Raize on course to Unity from the far side of the planet. They had made a rookie error in deploying every ship at the planet's disposal to this mission - Unity was now defenceless. They had succeeded in destroying the swarm, but what they hadn't anticipated was a smaller shoal of Raize that had approached Unity from her far-side. The enemy were deceptively wily, and tactically savvy. They knew the sheer panic that their mere appearance would cause, and they had anticipated what the response from Unity would be.

"Nataalu will have made a contingency plan," said Taire.

"She has," said Thirty-Two, "They have gone to the Unity Spire to prepare."

"No!" yelled Tecta, "She must not activate the Spire. The Raize feed on planetary energy. The Spire would only super-charge them."

"If the Spire can't save Unity, then what can?" said Taire.

"The Sixth Child of The Unity. I need to get down there to warn them."

"But, how?"

"Taire, I can withstand the journey through space as you well know. However, I don't have the required thrust or propulsion to get there in time."

"Bleep blurp."

"Clint, that's absurd."

"Wait, what did he say?"

"He suggested that we launch you from the Weapons Array."

"That's not as absurd as it first sounds. It could actually work."

"Bleept, blunk braarp, bleept." Clint blurted out a frenzied mess of sounds which cut through the panic.

"What did he say now, Taire?"

"He said, or you could hail Unity, and ask someone to pass on the message."

"That makes good sense. I think even us

Protector Droids are feeling the toll of this mission. My decision making may be a little off."

"Taire to Unity command, do you read me?" His hail was met with silence and static. "Unity, can you hear me?" he repeated. A long moment passed, and a voice finally answered.

"This is Unity command, we are receiving you," came an unfamiliar voice through the comms.

"I need you to get an urgent message to Nataalu. She must not activate the Unity Spire, under any circumstances!"

"But... they have already journeyed there. It might be our last hope..."

"No! If she activates it, it will be the last thing that she, or any of us, ever does."

"Understood. I will dispatch a messenger immediately."

"Please hurry. There is no time to waste."

The last of The Raize had been destroyed by the combined efforts of the allied fleets, but what should have been a rapturous celebration, was instead a muted, hollow victory.

"All vessels set a course to Unity - maximum thrust. We have to at least try to get back and help," Seventeen commanded. The entire fleet was submerged under a thick cloud of anxious tension. They sped towards home; all of them thinking the same thing, though no one dared to say the words. What if they were all too late?

Chapter Twenty-Eight

Stick Or Twist

Pilot had done exactly as The Nothing had asked. He had delivered The Seeker to Feer'aal's first moon, and had been static, waiting impatiently on the Core Loway ever since. He wasn't the only one who had grown impatient. He had been asked;

"Why we no move?" at least fifty times in the last thirty minutes. His fellow Pilots were behaving like children who were driving a parent insane on a long journey, except the question was, "Pilot, we go now?", instead of the usual, "Are we there yet?" He finally lost his temper.

"No more dis asking," he yelled. "Pilot wait for No thing tell Pilot go." As soon as Pilot's outburst had passed, the other Pilots and Pilot himself - erupted into roars of uncontrollable laughter. Tears of joy streamed down their faces. An enraged Pilot was one of the most ridiculous sights in the galaxy.

"Pilot sorry, friend Pilots. Pilot bored of wait, now we go."

"Go where?" croaked Co-Pilot.

"Pilot not know, let Loway decide." Pilot reached for the controls, but as he did so, the Loway burst into life. It gathered momentum so quickly that all of the Pilots in the control room were thrown backwards into the rear bulkhead.

"Pilot, what happens?" asked the stout
Pilot.

"Pilot think dis signal from The No
thing," Pilot replied.

"Where dis No thing take Pilots now?" said
the rotund Pilot.

"Pilot not know. You Pilot watch dis one,"
Pilot gestured to Nel's still lifeless body.
"Pilot look Loway route."

Chapter Twenty-Nine

The Messenger

Greem Greem Tah had made himself invisible since the first activation of the Unity Spire. He wasn't one who liked to stand out, he liked to keep himself to himself as much as possible. Now as he tore out of Unity command, pushing his antiquated landspeeder to its limit. He was exactly where he'd rather not be; right back in the mix. Instead of joining the fleet, he had stayed behind on Unity to mind Vrin. In the five years of peace that had followed the battle of Mora, she had grown even younger than she was on the day of that famous victory. He was now, in effect, her wet nurse. Despite the sudden unrest in restarting her aging process, it wasn't happening quickly enough for her to be self-sufficient, let alone being able to help in anyway. Greem Greem Tah was covering the rough terrain at a breakneck pace, but scores of unfamiliar shadows had appeared, creeping eerily over the landscape. He looked skyward and *BOOM*! An explosive roar thundered up ahead. The ripples of the ensuing energy wave toppled him from his speeder. From his newly-enforced vantage point (sprawled out, flat on his back), he witnessed the power and majesty of the activated Unity Spire. A column of light and energy ripped into the sky. He scrambled back to his feet, shaking off the dull-headedness caused by the impact of his fall. He climbed back onto his speeder, whose systems were still idling. *They don't make them like this anymore* he said to himself, engaging full thrust. He needed to stop the Children of The Unity before the threat of The Raize got even worse than it already was.

* * * * * * * * *

"Something's wrong!" screamed Lu, trying to make herself heard over the roar of energy erupting from the Spire. "They should've been destroyed on contact with the energy stream, but they are drifting on it - like they are playing..."

"Stay focused, we have to keep trying," replied Gliis.

"Nataalu!" shouted Greem Greem Tah, "You have to stop the activation!"

"Greem, what are you doing here? We cannot stop, because then we will be defenceless!!"

"The Unity Spire will make them stronger. They feed on planetary energy; it's like providing them with a tapped vein, feeding them directly from the planet's core."

"But, some have already made landfall. Look around, the trees, they are withering and dying. The colours are draining from the minerals of the rocks and we have no other defence."

The vibrant colours of the Unitian landscape were indeed paling all around them. The Raize were literally sucking the life out of the planet.

"Nataalu, you must listen to me. The order to stop the activation comes from Taire and Tecta."

Lu instantly broke her connection with the

group and the Spire.

"Tecta is back?" The shock in her voice was audible as she approached Greem. Tam, Gliis and Kee'Pah followed close behind, leaving an energy stream to recede into the Spire.

"Yes, they are on their way here now. The Raize have out-maneuvered the fleet with a second attack. We have to try ~~to~~ and stop them, but the Unity Spire is not the answer."

"What alternative do we have? We have no weapons."

"I came prepared." Greem took a munitions pack from his speeder, and armed all four of them with blasters. "Shoot any that come close to the Spire - we must not let them connect with it."

"Will this work against them?" asked Tam, referring to the basic blaster he'd been handed.

"There's only one way to find out," said Greem, and he opened fire on the bizarre creatures that littered the skies. Destroying the airborne creatures was simple enough, however the ones that had attached themselves to the surface were an entirely different prospect.

"If we can't break them free of the surface, this battle is over. Tam, Gliis - keep clearing them out of the skies. Greem, Kee'Pah, with me. Concentrate all fire on the land-sucking demons."

An otherworldly scream rang out in the mist... a Raize had been ripped from the planet's surface. However, it wasn't their relentless blaster fire that had released the planet from it's grasp. To the shock and surprise of the entire group, it was one of Pilot's Hornets that had broken its grip. The Children of The Unity watched on in disbelief, as dozens upon dozens of Raize were detached and destroyed by the Hornets. The vicious little machine's attacks were being launched to the surface by Unity's core. The raw energy that propelled them super-charged their deadly attacks, brutally blasting the enemy from the surface and throwing them high into the air, where they were finished off by the Hornet's ferocious core drills. A chorus of chilling, horrific screams provided the soundtrack for the Pilot's assault. The sound was so heart-wrenchingly hideous; it was nearly impossible not to feel the pain of these creatures. They were after all, in the most basic terms, just trying to fulfil the purpose of their existence.

The battle took a bizarre turn. The few Raize that had come into contact with the Unity Spire's energy stream - had mutated. They began to defend themselves; monstrous tendrils extended from their underside, and whipped viciously at the Hornets. Some succeeded in wrapping around the small assault crafts, and proceeded to launch them off in all directions - smashing some of them into the planet's surface. The sight of The Raize retaliating brought with it a renewed sense of panic, which rapidly replaced the group's short-lived feelings of hope.

Nataalu looked skyward. The sun appeared as a perfect white disc in the sky, but it's powerful life-giving rays struggled to penetrate the haze of silver ash that hung in the air. For the first time in many years, Nataalu and Gliis felt completely helpless,

unable to affect anything. This feeling
stirred up the long-forgotten memories of The
Husheds' invasion of Nataalu's mind, back on
Veela VI so many years before. Tam broke the
stunned silence.

    "Concentrate, and keep firing. Pilots are
doing their job, we need to do ours."

    "Tam is right. Those little ships are nigh
on indestructible, but they need our help."
said Lu.

Things rapidly deteoriated. A giant Raize
loomed over The Unity. The huge entity
completely obscured the sun. All five of them
directed their fire at the descending monster;
their blaster bolts burned with a luminous
intensity in the sprawling blanket of the
creature's dark shadow. The being's newly-
acquired tentacles thrashed violently through
the misty air. A multitude of plasma bolts
thumped into the creature, but it was too
dense to penetrate. The mutation triggered by
the planetary energy stream had not only
weaponized The Raize, but it had also
thickened their skin, and made them far less
vulnerable to conventional weapons. All felt
lost... it seemed like the hard-won battles,
the casualties, and all the hardships that
they had endured, were for nothing. Had they
saved anything?...

Chapter Thirty

A Child Of The Unity

The planet Unity was unrecognisable; shrouded in a silvery grey haze that lurked just below the atmosphere. Flashes lit up underneath the clouds and mist, as the conflict below raged on. The returning fleet had only been able to watch on, as the colossal energy stream of the Unity Spire had receded into the clouds and faded away.

"Are we too late?" asked Taire, tears already welling in his eyes.

"Do not lose hope just yet son," Tecta replied. The rest of the fleet hung back, watching edgily as The Hope and the Seeker descended cautiously through the thick ashen fog, where swirling plumes of ash spiralled in their wake.

"The whole atmosphere is filled with the ashes of The Raize. Someone down here has been fighting back to cause this much debris," said Taire. Although visibility was poor, they could hear the uniquely familiar sound of thrust engines.

"Tecta! Hornets! Pilots must have done this damage." As the haze cleared, their attention was immediately drawn to the Unity Spire. A heart-breaking scene came into view; where a gargantuan Raize hovered over the Children of The Unity, poised, ready to crush them, and suck all life out of the planet via the Unity Spire. Taire was about to squeeze the trigger on the weapons array - when something else happened. The Raize erupted into the now familiar ash that covered the planet. Pilot's Hornet emerged from the cloud of remains. He had punched a hole clean through its centre, causing the mammoth being to disintegrate before their eyes.

"Pilots, finish dis things." Pilot's command to the Hornets came through on The Seeker's open comms channel.

The Children of The Unity and Greem were caked in a thick layer of ashen-silver remains. They blinked through the falling flakes and powder to see the very welcome sight of The Hope, The Seeker and the Hornets clearing out the remaining Raize. Taire turned to Tecta and said,

"I don't understand. You said the Sixth Child of The Unity would save them."

"I did, and he has," Tecta replied.

"I don't follow. You are the original child of Unity. The Sixth to be found, but the First to be created."

"Open your eyes Taire. It was never me. Pilot is the Sixth, he just doesn't know it yet."

"When do you plan on telling him?"

"All in good time, there is no rush," Tecta smiled.

The Seeker and The Hope set down close to the Spire. No sooner had the hatch opened - Tecta and Taire were immediately embraced by Lu and Gliis.'

"I'm so glad you are home and safe," said Nataalu.

"I'm relieved we still have a home to come back to," Taire replied.

"Did you see Pilot save us from that monstrous beast?" exclaimed Gliis.

"I did brother. He is a constant source of surprise," said Taire, who gave Tecta a knowing look.

Greem wore a dejected expression as he surveyed the scene around them.

"So what happens now?" he asked. "Everything looks so lifeless and ruined."

"We will rebuild," was Nataalu's defiant response.

* * * * * * * * * *

The Council members had gathered in the Great Hall. The room was alive with vibrant, hopeful voices. Despite the carnage The Raize had caused, the gathered were in high spirits. This had been a win; a messy win, but a win nonetheless. They chatted amongst small groups - in anticipation of Nataalu's address to the whole of the New Unity.

Seventeen and Zero-Nine were huddled in heated debate.

"I will deliver the news to Tecta in person," said Seventeen sternly.

"But, I took the initiative and performed the scans," Zero protested.

"You also choose to behave like a tactless Slengraap. It is not up for debate," snapped Seventeen.

"Thunder stealer," sniped Zero, as he walked away in disgust.

Seventeen approached Tecta, Taire, Gliis, Tam and Kee'Pah. The group were in the midst of a long, overdue catch up.

"Tecta, sorry to interrupt. May I speak with you?"

"Of course Seventeen."

"It is a sensitive matter."

"Anything you say to me can be said in the presence of my children."

"When we passed over Feer'aal, Zero-Nine, (in his boredom), took the liberty of scanning the planet. There were numerous lifeforms present on the surface. All biological signatures suggest that they are indeed Feruccian."

This was a bittersweet moment for Tecta.

"I am indeed very grateful that I am not responsible for genocide, however, this means there is yet another threat that we must take care not to ignore. They will be out for revenge."

"Before you concern yourself with ifs and buts, allow yourself to enjoy a moment of peace, old friend."

"You should listen to him Tecta," said Taire. Tecta gave a faint smile - Seventeen knew him too well. It felt good to be home amongst family and friends.

Nataalu approached the podium. She cleared her throat and commanded the room's full attention.

"Friends and allies. I hope we can all agree that we have learned a valuable lesson. Since the battle of Mora, we had become complacent, too passive and self-assured. Look around you. Our planet has paid the price for our failings. There is an ever-present darkness that endures in our galaxy... deep-seeded and evil. We have turned a blind eye, hoping our mission for peace would be enough to convert, or at least keep them down. As we go forward, we must strike a balance between the peace for which we strive, and self-preservation. We need to accept that this darkness endures, and we must learn to understand our enemy, and keep them at bay. Our growth and survival depend on it. The sentient planets have awakened; we cannot, and will not, jeopardise the support of the sentient planets, and the real hope that that support brings. We will be united amongst ourselves, and unified with other worlds. We will move forwards together! For peace!"

"Those were very wise words from a true leader," said Tecta.

Chapter Thirty-One

On The Core Loway

It had been two days since the invasion, and
Taire had worked tirelessly on Nel's systems.
He had integrated the Tek into her core
programming, and had run every possible
diagnostic/scenario. It was time to wake her.
Clint remained unconvinced that waking Nel up
was a good idea. He had been ordered to stand
guard over her, and he was one hundred percent
focused on ensuring that Nel stayed
deactivated. Taire activated the boot
sequence, and waited...

As soon as Nel stirred, a static hiss and
crackle sounded. Clint had zapped her with a
static charge, to return her to an unconscious
state. The diminutive droid wasn't taking any
chances. The savagery in Nel's intent to kill
Tecta had left him on the edge of neurosis.
    "Clint, why did you do that? I need to
wake her up," Taire snapped in disbelief.
Clint replied with a short bleep.
    "You panicked?"
    "Blruupt."
    "She did not look at you funny. Stop
making excuses!"
    "Blunkt." Clint made a remorseful sound.
    "Sorry? So you should be. Now undo what
you just did. Wake her up." Clint gave a
series of severe bleeps.

"Of course I'm sure she's fixed." Clint made a defeated groaning sound, and begrudgingly did as Taire asked. He woke Nel with an energy charge - the droid equivalent of an adrenaline shot.

Nel's gentle green eyes opened groggily.

"Nel, it's okay, it's me Taire. Are you...yourself?"

"Of course I am myself! What kind of question is that?"

"The Dark Mother, she was controlling you..." Nel's eyes snapped wide open, her expression full of panic.

"No!" she cried, "I hoped it was a bad dream, a system glitch. I am so sorry Taire. I was powerless to stop her. I felt like a spectator in my own body. But, it's only now that her voice and presence have fallen silent, that I realise she was always there in the background. Ever since I killed those poor Raktarians and shut myself down."

"It's okay Nel, she can't use you anymore. But I need you to think. Do you remember anything about her?"

"I saw the place where she dwells... a phase planet. She called it Po'Tu. She has conquered the planet, and has amassed an army. She is single-minded in her pursuit of control. All she desires is death and destruction. She craves total power through annihilation. Taire, she is coming for us all..."

The End

Epilogue

Won'Kaat Station

"What brings you here, stranger?" said the gruff bar-keep. He was a sturdy man, who was a mess of scruffy hair and bad breath.

"New Unity business," Treelo replied. "I am an ambassador, here to spread the word of peace to the darker parts of the galaxy."

"I'd keep that quiet round these parts if I were you. You could attract yourself a whole lot of trouble."

"Well, a little trouble isn't so bad. It gives me an excuse to stay amongst the 'action', if you get my meaning."

"You are certainly an unusual type for this part of the galaxy. Our establishment offers undertaking services, if you want to plan ahead."

"I don't think that'll be necessary. Do you know anything of Kan Vok Tah? I heard he is here abouts."

"Kan Vok Tah? Are you here for revenge or drugs? It's always one of the two."

"Well, he's my father." The bar-keep raised a curious eyebrow.

"Just kidding, neither of those reasons. I'm just fulfilling my civic duty as an ambassador to the New Unity."

"Does that civic duty include running up a gigantic Raktee tab?"

"Perks of the job - I get expenses paid. I'm an ambassador, not a saint," he laughed.

"Even if I did know where he is, I'm not stupid enough to tell you, or anyone else. You don't meddle with Kan Vok Tah."

"Huh hmm, pardon my rude interruption, I couldn't help but overhear that you are an ambassador of the New Unity. I for one would like to learn more of the wonders that are being done in the name of peace."

"I appreciate your interest friend. I am Treelo, and you are?"

"My name is Daa'Shond…"

The Unity Chronicles
will continue

Book Four

The Essence

This book is dedicated to my wife Lisa, my children Louis and Annabelle. To my family and friends who have supported my work and of course anyone who has read my books x

Cover art by Graham Mann

Printed in Great Britain
by Amazon